HERE
BE
DRAGONS

CAROLYN
DALE

Here Be Dragons
Carolyn Dale

Copyright Carolyn Dale 2017

Carrick Publishing
Print Edition 2017
ISBN 13: 978-1-77242-064-7
Cover Design by Sara Carrick

Author's Note

To the people in Drumheller, Alberta who asked me when I was going to set a mystery in their town, here it is! I have changed the name and some of the geography, but the Royal Tyrell Museum and the hoodoos are still here, even though I have not used the name of the museum. The inmates can be happy that I made the prison disappear and replaced it with an agricultural college.

Carolyn Dale is a pen name of
mystery author Anne Barton.

www.annebartonmysteries.ca
www.mysterycarolyndale.ca

CHAPTER ONE

"Where's the Alberta map?"

I stuck my head out of the bathroom of our motel room and saw my husband rummaging in a drawer of the nightstand beside the bed.

"Have you looked in the car? Maybe you took it back out after we used it yesterday."

"Gail, I looked there. I can't find it anywhere."

I wrapped my bathrobe around my still damp body and came out to join the search, but neither of us could find the map.

"Oh well," I shrugged. "We can pick up another on our way. We'll have to stop for gas somewhere and the service station should have maps. Besides, we won't fall off the edge of the earth if we don't find one. There will be road signs."

Anton grinned. "Do you remember those old maps from medieval times—those ones that show old sailing ships falling off the edge of the world?"

"Yes. And the comment beside them, 'Here be Dragons!'"

He gave me a hug and a quick peck on the cheek. "If we don't find a map, we'll just have to be on the lookout for dragons."

We stopped in Regina on our way from Guelph, where Anton had just received his PhD in agronomy. He was to take up a new position at an agricultural college in Drayford, Alberta. I had gotten my Doctor of Veterinary Medicine degree at Guelph the year before and just finished a year of internship. I was to run an emergency veterinary clinic in the booming town that had been transformed three years before by the opening of Drayford Agricultural College. The college had grown so fast, it was decided to expand it into a full-scale, degree granting university. The faculty would nearly double in size over that with which the college started. There was a good possibility that Anton would be granted an assistant professorship within a year or two.

I had no idea how busy the veterinarians had become with all this expansion. I only knew that they decided to pool their resources and set up an emergency clinic to give themselves time off from their workload.

Anton received several offers, choosing Drayford over his second choice, a provincial laboratory that was studying plant diseases. Anton is a plant geneticist, and they wanted him. So, out of curiosity, we stopped in Regina to visit the lab. After the visit, Anton had second thoughts about his decision. The lab really interested him, and I knew that I could get a job as a vet in either place. But then, he rationalized, once he got to Drayford, he might have the same reaction to the position there. He was committed for a year, so we were ready to go on and embrace our new adventure.

For both of us, it was our first venture into full-time employment. We were both nervous and excited at the prospect. To add to the feeling of new beginnings, we were married the day after my internship ended and spent a few days in Gananoque, the gate to the Thousand Islands, for our honeymoon before setting out on our new life. We were Ontarians by birth and education, with no idea about what prairie life would be like. Map or no map, I had a feeling that we might indeed be falling off the edge of our world.

We hoped our old Pontiac Vibe, stuffed with belongings and pulling a small rental trailer, would last through the journey. So far, so good! We hadn't had any trouble and one more day would bring us to the end of our journey.

From Regina, we headed northwest, finally picking up an east-west highway and approaching the Alberta border. We stopped for gas, but found the service station had run out of maps. We pushed on. The road did not stop when we came to a sign announcing our entry into Alberta. It just rolled out ahead of us in a straight line as far as the eye could see, the distant reaches shimmering in the summer sun. The cool of early morning departed and the temperature climbed steadily. My lips were drying out and I rummaged in the glove compartment for a tube of Chapstick. We didn't have air conditioning in the old heap, so the windows were rolled down. Anton's left arm was resting on the frame of the open window, and as the sun moved southward, he complained that his skin began to sting from the sunburn. We had been told that the dry air on the prairies would be more comfortable than the sticky humidity we were used to, but I was discovering that dry air presents a different set of problems.

We changed drivers, having agreed that each of us would drive a two-hour segment. Eventually we came to an intersection with a large sign and an arrow pointing to our left. Drayford, 20km.

"I don't see anything that looks like a town," Anton muttered as I turned onto the new road. We could see across the flat land to the south for far more than twenty kilometres and could see no sign of anything other than the alternating wheat and canola fields, with an occasional grassy pasture where cattle grazed.

"I don't either, but I've discovered that distances look different out here where the air is so dry. I'm always underestimating."

"Well, we'll soon find out."

Knowing that our destination was so near, I had a tendency to put my foot down on the accelerator. Then I'd check the speedometer and have to slow down to a decent speed. I hadn't checked the odometer when I turned onto this road, but it seemed as if we had gone at least twenty kilometres and could see no sign of a town. We should be getting there. Did I read that sign correctly?

Suddenly the road disappeared over the brink of a deep gash across the flat prairie. I slammed on the brake, but remembering the trailer, let up and braked more carefully, as we passed a sign saying, Viewpoint 200m. I pulled in and stopped the car on what seemed to be the edge of a precipice. Anton walked around from the passenger side, noticing the cracking sound from the engine as it began to cool.

"At least this buggy can coast the rest of the way if she quits on us now."

We turned our attention to the panorama spread out before us. A lazy river had, over millions of years, cut a deep valley through the desert, baring multiple layers of sediment, each one defining a particular phase of the evolution of the prairie landscape. At the bottom, a wide spread of level land flanked the river on both sides. There lay the community of

Drayford, dreaming peacefully in the afternoon sun. Updrafts of heat rising from the valley walls, created a gentle breeze, which seemed to carry up with it the sounds of the town. There was a background hum of traffic, the occasional sharper report from some construction activity and the occasional shout from one of the children splashing in a pool of the river below overhanging willows. They could be seen only as faint dots or splashes on the surface of the water. As well as distance being deceptive, it appeared that the dry, still air enhanced distant sounds.

Half way up the opposite valley wall, a group of white buildings revealed the location of the new college. Houses were sprouting on the bare hillside between the college and the town. A new shopping mall occupied a level bench. The starkness of this new construction contrasted sharply with the muted tones of tree-lined streets of the older part of town.

Anton put an arm around my shoulders and pressed me close to him. "I hope you're going to like it."

I smiled up at him. "Let's go see it close up."

Anton, now driving, descended the grade into town in a lower gear to save the brakes. We crossed an old steel bridge, painted light blue. The highway divided into one-way streets as we entered the downtown area. Newly erected traffic lights impeded the flow of traffic and we progressed in fits and starts until the streets joined again and became the highway up the other side of the valley. "I wonder whether they will build a bypass around the town."

"They'll have to. I suppose this congestion is all because of the rapid growth."

"I suppose so."

We passed a massive new mall and headed up the side of the valley. Soon a left turn collection lane appeared, accompanied by a sign pointing left and directing us to the college. Up a short drive the road leveled, passed through a gate and divided at a massive fountain. Anton hesitated, but then remembered. "They said to go left at the fountain and drive all the way around to the far end." As the car passed beside the fountain, I glanced out my open window at three massive creatures spouting streams of water into the air. The water hung briefly before dropping into the surrounding pool.

"Stop!"

Anton slammed on the brake. "What…?"

"Look. Here be Dragons!"

CHAPTER TWO

The dragons were explained as we drove around the lower side of a loop, with college buildings on either side, the street light standards decorated by banners in red and gold, with prancing dragons surrounded by the name Drayford Dragons. The college nickname, no doubt.

We found the Administration Building and went in. Entering what seemed to be the office, we were greeted warmly by two smiling middle-aged ladies who introduced themselves as Marge and Sandra. Marge further described herself as President Beliveau's personal secretary. After they had welcomed Anton as a new faculty member, they turned to me.

"You must be the new vet who is going to operate an emergency clinic," Marge exclaimed shaking my hand. "Do you go by your maiden name, or are you now another Dr. Schild?"

I was impressed that she had picked up the proper pronunciation of Anton's last name. "I'll use my maiden name, McKinnon, since that is the name on my diploma and on my licenses."

7

Sandra wanted to be sure of the name. "You pronounce it 'Shield,' do you?" she asked.

"That's right." Anton smiled at her. "Lots of people get it wrong, and when I tell them to pronounce it 'Shield' they almost always say 'Shields.' Otherwise, people often pronounce it 'Shilled.' I've given up correcting people."

"You know, I had pictured you as a small, middle-aged man with black hair and a goatee, wearing glasses on a chain." She viewed Anton's six feet of well-muscled frame, topped by light brown almost blond hair.

Anton laughed. "That would be my great grandfather. He was a student in Vienna in the nineteen thirties, who got into trouble with Hitler's government over his political views and had to get out of Austria. He also was a member of a theatre troupe, and was playing the role of an alienist, which is what psychiatrists were called in those days, so he put on his makeup when they left for a tour of Switzerland and France, and got by the police who were looking for him. From France, he went to England and asked for asylum. He met an attractive young woman, a teacher, married her and got her pregnant—not necessarily in that order..."

That got a laugh from everyone.

"They heard about jobs in Canada and got passage on the last regular sailing of an ocean liner before the start of the war. My grandfather was born in Halifax just after they arrived. They found work as teachers in the Ottawa area. My grandfather grew up there and married a farmer's daughter, so I have both teaching and farming in my background. So it's appropriate that I end up teaching at an agricultural college."

"Your family must retain ties to Austria. Anton is not a common name here," Marge remarked.

"We have retained ties to family in the old world. There is an Anton in every generation of the Schild family. I happen to be it in this generation."

"Oh! Here comes Mrs. Beliveau. Nancie, meet one of our new faculty members, Dr. Anton Schild, and his wife, Dr. McKinnon."

Nancie Beliveau, a tall, slender lady with a graceful gait and lustrous auburn hair in an attractive upswept hairdo, approached us with hand outstretched to shake ours. "Welcome to Drayford. I hope you will like it here, both of you. I see you have just married. But you are retaining your maiden name," she said in a pleasantly modulated voice. I explained again my reason for doing so.

"I wish you well in your new enterprise. Guy and I have a Bichon, who is a handful, but we love him. So we may see you in that capacity one of these days."

"I hope not," I replied. "That would mean you had an emergency with him."

She laughed. "I hope we don't see you in your professional capacity, but with our pup, you never know! At any rate, I hope to get to know you both and I hope you become involved with college activities."

"She will if Della Virtue gets hold of her," Sandra remarked.

"Oh dear, yes." Nancie Beliveau explained, "Della is the wife of our treasurer, Sam Virtue. And if you want advice on where to find an accountant or a financial advisor, talk to Sam. He only works for the college, but he knows all the others in his field. His advice is quite sound. You will meet everyone at the President's Reception on Thursday, if you haven't already met them. By the way, the reception is as close as we get to a formal function. It's not formal, but you should show up in suit and tie for the men and your best clothes for the women. No jeans or bare midriffs. At other times, we're quite informal."

"I look forward to it," Anton replied, obviously a bit overwhelmed by the reception he was receiving. I had a feeling of relief. We were going to be happy here, if today was an indication of things to come.

Anton collected a key and instructions on where to find our unit in the faculty housing, which was on a side road leading off the ring road we had just come on. We found our unit on the end of a row of townhouses. On the other side of the road was the married student housing. The dorms were farther along the road. We had seen a mobile home park outside the boundary of the campus, and on the other side of the entrance road, a development of mid-size single-family homes, some under construction. We were to find that almost everyone on campus lived in some sort of campus housing. The town of Drayford was overwhelmed by the rapid expansion of the college, and there was no housing available in town.

Anton backed the trailer onto one of the parking spaces at our new home, parked the Vibe in the other one, and we entered by the back door. The ground floor consisted of a great room, designed to serve as living room and dining area, and a kitchen with a storage area off of it that also held a stacked washer and dryer. Upstairs there were two bedrooms and the bathroom. We had asked for a furnished unit as we had few items of furniture. Most of what we brought with us consisted of boxes of books, our hi-fi equipment and our stripped down bicycles.

The furniture was sturdy and functional, and certainly not decorative. I wondered if it had been bought from Army surplus.

Tired from our journey, we decided not to unload the trailer at this time, but to go out to dinner. The ladies had recommended several eateries to us, with different types of food. We chose the barbecue establishment and ate a hearty meal. On returning to our new home, we took our sleeping bags from the back of the car and slung them on the bed in the first bedroom we came to, dropped into bed and slept soundly.

CHAPTER THREE

Anton is an early bird. He gets up at five, rain or shine, wherever we are. So since the next part of our indoctrination occurred while I was still sound asleep, I'll let him tell you about it.

At five, the sun was already up and the cool of the night was rapidly dissipating. I like to go for either a run or a bike ride first thing in the morning. The bikes were still in the trailer, in pieces, so it was a run this morning. I started along the ring road in the direction we had gone the day before. There were already maintenance workers busily at their jobs. I stopped to talk to one.

"We do our work early so as not to interfere with classes and such. We can't use power tools until seven."

"This is Sunday. Do you work every day?"

"You bet. Hey! If you go around to the side of the Ad building, there's a door to the basement and there's always coffee on in there."

"Thanks. I'll look in on them."

I followed the man's advice, found the entry to the basement, and was greeted by two of the janitors who offered me coffee and were quite willing to answer questions. From them I learned the campus routine. Where to go for refreshments (don't miss the dairy bar), how to find the tennis courts and gym (it opens at six because a lot of kids want to get in some workouts before they go to class), and who was who among the college staff. They also ran the lost and found (it's amazing what these kids manage to lose) they told me.

The top side of the ring was where the shops that sold the foodstuffs raised at the college were located. The first one I came to was the dairy bar. Going around to the back door, as I had been instructed, I was admitted to the working part of a dairy operation. I introduced myself and was offered a mug of hot chocolate. "The best you'll ever get," I was told. I had to agree. It was made with half-and-half and topped by a mound of whipped cream that did not come out of a spray can. Two young men were busy making ice cream. "Ours is very popular. People from town come up here to buy ice cream and cheese. And we supply all the dairy products for the college.

"We run a regular dairy farm here. It's up on the top where the prairie starts. There are pastures for the cows, a milking parlour, and the milk goes into a storage tank just like any other dairy farm. We have our own tanker truck that brings the milk down here to us. The driver tests the milk before loading it into the truck, same as any commercial operation. All the work is done by students, except for a few experienced staff like myself. These other two guys here this morning are students who are hired for summer jobs. They do everything, including driving and cleaning the truck. But when the truck needs maintenance, it goes to agricultural engineering for the students there to work on it. Nobody gets to be lazy on this campus."

The next person I found at work that morning was a grizzled older man, uncovering a display of the college farm's produce. There were heaps of peppers, huge heads of lettuce and cabbage, rows of carrots and beets, and piles of onions and potatoes. They all looked perfect, as if someone had painted a picture of beautiful bounty. I expressed my appreciation.

"Pretty good, eh? This is the stuff produced by modern farming methods. That over there…" he pointed to another table still covered by moistened burlap "…is the organic garden stuff."

I had to laugh. He was so obviously championing his produce over that of his competition.

"They're so picky, they made the college give them land as far away from ours as possible, so ours won't contaminate their stuff. They even have to have their own bees, for fear a bee from our hives might stray over their way. They even think their honey is better than ours 'cause ours might make people into some sort of freak. But people buy ours 'cause it's cheaper. We put our plants in the ground and water them and they grow. We don't need any insecticides 'cause the plants are engineered to resist all the bugs that prey on them. It's better for the environment, too"

"I know that this college is very much into GMO research. That's why they hired me."

"You bet. It's the way to go. Look at this stuff! Hey, are you the new guy in agronomy who is supposed to be the expert on genetics?"

"That's me, but I don't know how expert I am as yet. I'm Dr. Anton Schild."

"I'm Barry." We shook hands.

"Have you met Kent Anderson?" he asked.

"Not yet. I just got here."

"He's a grad student from the U of Alberta who's on loan to us to run this organic operation. He's a real fanatic."

"I expect I'll meet him soon."

"He complains that the college prices his stuff higher than this here. But that's Mendel's class in the math department who set the prices. They figure out what it costs to grow the stuff and then figure what it ought to sell for."

"That sounds practical."

"Yeah. He has his class do that with everything on the farm."

None of the other shops or stands were open yet, so I next found myself at the Dragon Fountain. The basin was empty of water and three men were busy cleaning it. Laid out on some sacking was an array of coins, mostly nickels and quarters with some loonies, a few rings and even one watch.

"Did these come out of the fountain," I asked.

"They did," one man told me. "You'd be amazed at what people throw into it or accidentally drop into it, like that watch. We even found a smart phone one time. You'd think that if someone dropped a phone, they'd try to fish it out."

"If they did, it wouldn't work. That's probably why they didn't bother."

"Yeah, but when I was growing up, we took better care of our property because if we lost it, tough luck. We couldn't afford to replace it. Kids today are a lot more casual about their things."

"What do you do with the booty?"

"You know, the first time we cleaned the fountain after it was put up, we asked ourselves that same question. We didn't think it was ours to divvy up. We took it to the president's office and asked if we could use what we collected to put on a

Christmas party for all the kiddies. A lot of the students have kids, and so do the profs and us workers. Pres thought that was a first rate idea. We've been doing that ever since, and we have enough for a spring picnic for the kids as well. We get all the food from the farm here, so it doesn't cost very much. And one of the animal husbandry students is a rodeo clown during the summer, so he put on a show for the kids. The rest of the stuff goes to lost and found."

"How come Dragons, not Dinosaurs, as a college nickname? This is dinosaur country."

"Oh, the U of Calgary got Dinos first, and the local high school team calls themselves Dinosaurs. The first year, the students were asked for suggestions and came up with some really weird names, like Mad Bulls and Grim Reapers. They took the three most common suggestions and held a vote. Dragons won."

"This is an impressive fountain. How did the college get it?"

"Some guy who donated the land for the college donated the fountain the next year. He won't let his name be used on anything, so it's just called the Dragon Fountain. Hey! I gotta get back to work. If we don't get done by seven, we'll get wet. The water gets shut off automatically at one and comes back on at seven. On Sundays, though, it not only shuts off at one, but automatically drains the pool so we can clean it."

I left the fountain and ran back to our new home.

While Anton was out getting acquainted with all the early morning workers, I received a call on my cell phone from my grandfather. Like Anton, he was an early bird, and to call at seven o'clock on a Sunday morning did not seem odd to him at all. I was up but not fully awake.

"Now that you have arrived in Drayford, I'll come and help you get settled in," he said. "You will need things like furniture and linens. Do you have anything to cook with?"

"I was living on my own for several years," I remind him. "And our townhouse is furnished."

"Are you sure the furniture is usable?"

"Of course it is. We slept on one of the beds last night and it didn't collapse."

"But you will need a lot of other things to make your house a home. I'm going to come over and take you shopping. I assume they do have Sunday shopping in Drayford."

"Don't come today Granddad," I replied, knowing that his visit was inevitable. "We haven't even unloaded the trailer yet. We need to do that and return the trailer to the rental place. Besides, I need to get together with the other vets. We have a lot to do."

"Okay, I'll come tomorrow. I'll take the early flight to Calgary and rent a car. I'll be there in the afternoon. In the meantime, start making a list of the things you need."

"Granddad, you don't need to buy things for us. We will now have two professional salaries."

"Can't I help my only granddaughter get started in her new life?"

"But at least wait till Tuesday to come. We have a lot of other stuff to do."

"All right. If you insist. I'll come Tuesday."

I love my granddad, but he can be a bit controlling. He is a retired Inspector of the RCMP, but his was not regular police work. He was the conductor of the RCMP Concert Band, back in the days it was in existence. He doesn't like to be called 'Inspector' because he then has to explain that he was not part of any investigation they happen to be asking about. Since my grandmother's death, he has moved to Victoria, where the weather is better than in the Barrie area of Ontario. But he doesn't know anyone and I'm sure he is lonely.

When Anton returned with his account of the people he met, I told him we'd better get unpacked and have everything in order, or Inspector McKinnon would take over our lives. I would arrange to meet the town's other vets Tuesday morning, before he arrived.

"By the way," I said, critically eyeing my husband, "I think it might be better if you don't go running around the campus here wearing a Guelph Gryphons T-shirt."

"Oh, sorry. I just grabbed the first shirt I could out of my bag. I'll retire the Gryphons."

CHAPTER FOUR

I scheduled a noon luncheon meeting with the town's other vets for Tuesday. We met at the new steakhouse in the big mall. But before I went to the meeting, I decided to drop in on the local SPCA. Humane societies and vets don't always have a good relationship, though they should, both being concerned with the well-being of animals. It is the business relationship that is the problem. Years ago, vets began to recommend spays and neuters for dogs and cats, not only for population control but for the well-being of the pets. They were so successful that they ended up losing a good part of their livelihood. Humane societies and private organization started hiring vets to do assembly-line spays and neuters at prices so low the established vets couldn't compete. Some humane societies have worked in combination with established vet clinics to the betterment of all concerned, but others have not.

I worked for a vet when I was in high school who was so incensed by the local humane society requiring all animals adopted from their shelter to be taken to one specific vet clinic for spays, neuters and vaccinations that he went to the city council to complain that since the humane society was partially funded by the city by way of tax relief, grants, and use of their shelter for impounded dogs, they should require the humane society to treat all veterinarians licensed in the city equally. He won.

I met the SPCA director and liked her instantly. We had a good conversation, and I came away with the feeling that she and I were going to get along quite well.

There were four veterinary practices in town. One had a big, sprawling building, luxuriously appointed, on the other side of the river. There were four vets, three partners and a new graduate, just starting. The senior partner, Alex Breling, was the representative for the group that I had contact with when applying for the job. I began to realize that Alex was one of those bossy types, who assume leadership that does not belong to them, and talk down anyone who disagrees.

A couple in their mid-thirties, the Donaldsons, both vets, had opened a clinic on the far side of the mall from the stores and restaurants when the new college had come to town. They were both tall and thin, serious and condescending. I envisioned them as vegetarians who rode bicycles to work in all weathers, and thought so-called 'Cadillac' medicine was the only way to go. It turned out that I was right on all counts. They ordered vegetarian lasagna while everyone else ordered the house's steaks.

Tom Grant, a man in his forties came with his wife, Betsy, who was his technician, receptionist, business manager, and sometimes kennel help. They were a matching pair but quite different from the other couple. Both were plump, smiling extroverts who greeted me warmly. Their clinic was on the outskirts of town, down the river, and was in the basement of their house. He was anticipating that their daughter would join the practice in a year, when she graduated from the vet school at the University of Saskatchewan. He was then planning on building a clinic on the property, which also included pastures and corrals for horses, cattle and goats. There were cats and dogs everywhere. I learned later that he had a practice as busy as the one with the four vets. His clients loved him, warming to his friendly ways and his wife's ability to make everyone feel welcome, to enthuse over their new puppies and kittens, and to console them if they had to have an elderly pet put down. He was a workaholic, and was available seven days a week.

The last of the vets, Irwin Prouse, came late and I noticed a definite change in the atmosphere when he entered. It was obvious that none of the other vets liked him. He was older, a sour faced, grumpy man who complained about everything from the steaks to the requirement that he donate to the fund that would pay my salary. "I won't be sending any cases to this emergency clinic, so why should I pay?"

"But we get emergency calls from people who couldn't get in touch with you, so unless you take all your emergency calls yourself, they will end up at the emergency clinic," Alex said. "So you need to pay up, like the rest of us."

It was Tom Grant who brought up the only really contentious issue we discussed at this meeting. It apparently wasn't the first time he had broached the subject.

"This is the time we should change the way we schedule our days on call," he said.

I had worked out a deal where I would work five nights, then have three nights off. On those nights, the other vets would work at the emergency clinic, on a rotation basis. They were already doing so on weekends, and had been for a couple of weeks.

"As it is now," Tom remarked, "each *clinic* in town takes the duty one night. There are two clinics with more than one vet. Those clinics should be in the rotation based on the number of *vets* in the clinic. Alex, your clinic takes one night out of every four, and I take one night out of every four. There should be eight nights in the rotation, not four."

Alex insisted that the current rotation should be continued, as did the Donaldson couple. I saw a look of horror on the face of the new young vet in Alex's practice, and realized that if the change were made, he'd be the one to take all four of that clinic's nights. I was sure that Alex and his two partners never took the emergency calls. I felt sorry for the young man, but I also agreed with Tom Grant.

After lunch, Alex escorted me to the storefront site of my new workplace. It was right in the downtown area and I wondered how they had gotten permission to operate a veterinary clinic in a business district. It seemed that the town had become worried by the many empty stores, as businesses moved to outlying malls, and conveniently failed to look at the city code that regulated where certain types of business could be located.

I looked with dismay at the scanty equipment, all of it discards from other clinics, that I would have to work with. I began to recite a list of other equipment and supplies that I would need.

"We don't have an unlimited budget," Alex complained.

"I know. But these are things that are essential. For example, how can I treat injured animals without having narcotics for pain?"

"There are other, non-controlled drugs for pain."

"Yeah. For chronic pain or mild discomfort, but you can't expect me to give an NSAID to a dog that has been hit by a car and has multiple fractures."

"I'll discuss it with the others," Alex replied.

The definite feeling I got was that, though my internship had concentrated on emergency medicine, and I felt confident in doing that, I had no experience in the type of business decisions I would have to make. It gave me a sinking feeling in the pit of my stomach.

We had unloaded the trailer on Sunday, returned it to the rental company, and started unpacking. Monday, we got nearly everything into cupboards or bookshelves. We called the phone company and ordered a phone. The college provided the other utilities. We decided to wait a while before connecting to the TV cable company. On Tuesday, Granddad flew to Calgary, rented a car and drove to Drayford. I had barely returned from my meeting when he showed up.

"I stopped on the way for lunch. I didn't want you to feel you had to fix anything for me. I also checked into that new Best Western. I don't want to saddle you with having to care for me while I'm here. And tonight, I'll take you both out to dinner. Now, let's make a list of what you need in this house." He began a room-by-room inspection, notebook in hand. What he came up with was far more luxurious than anything we had planned.

"Granddad, we are trying to live frugally until we are established and have paid off our student loans. We don't need all this stuff."

"Don't worry about the cost. I'm paying for this. I helped my grandsons get started out and now I want to do the same for my only granddaughter."

Realizing that once he made up his mind, nothing would deter Inspector McKinnon from doing what he wanted, I capitulated.

"Tomorrow, we go shopping," he said firmly.

While I was getting acquainted with my new colleagues, Anton put in his first appearance at the Agronomy department, was shown the lecture rooms and the labs, his own small office, and met his fellow faculty members. As he described to it me, when he was leaving in the late afternoon and retrieving his bike, he was hailed by an energetic middle-aged woman who stood in his path and demanded attention.

"I'm Della Virtue. I am the chair of the faculty wives. We meet every month to plan our activities. Our first meeting is Friday evening at five-thirty at my house. It's potluck. Tell your wife to bring a hot dish or salad for the potluck. Too many of the girls bring desserts. We go by first names. What's your wife's name?"

Anton gathered his wits and finally answered. "She won't be interested, I don't think."

"Well she should. All the faculty wives belong."

"Besides she works that night."

"Tell her to get off work early. It's important that she come."

"She can't get off work. She has her own profession. She isn't just a 'faculty wife.' She has obligations."

"I'm sure if she tries, she can get her boss to let her off. It's important."

"She is her own boss."

"Then she can take off whenever she wants to. What's her name?"

"No she can't. Her name is Dr. Gail McKinnon and she runs the veterinary emergency clinic."

"Surely she can find someone to fill in for her."

"No she *can't.*" Anton was getting frustrated, trying to get away from the woman. Finally someone came along and spoke to him and he managed to walk off with them, wheeling his bike.

When he told me his tale, I had a good laugh, but then I had a second thought. "I hope that my refusing to get involved won't put you in some sort of difficulty with the college authorities."

"I can't see how it would."

It was the first negative incident in our introduction to college life.

CHAPTER FIVE

I had just returned from shopping with Granddad when our new phone rang. Anton picked up the phone, said hello, and then waited with a pained expression to a long exposition by the person on the other end of the line. She apparently asked for Dr. Schild and when he asked, "Which Dr. Schild?" he gave me a wink. When he could get in another word, I heard him say, "Oh, you need to talk to my wife." He handed me the phone.

"This is Dr. Gail Schild," I said, having taken my cue from Anton. "How can I help you?"

"Oh, I'm so worried about my Max. He won't eat and he's losing weight and he has to do number one every hour or two, but he can't do number two at all, and he complains all the time, and I'm sure he's in pain because he always just sits there and does nothing. I think he must have that awful thing, you know, the one that starts with C, because I remember when his mother had it in one of her—uh—you know what I mean, and she just lay around and wouldn't eat, and she died…"

"Wait a minute." I almost had to yell into the phone in order to be heard over her high-pitched complaints. "I'm not in private practice. I will be running the emergency clinic."

"But I have to see you because all the other doctors have given up on him and don't know what's the matter with him and I don't want to take him back to any of them. I was so glad to hear that there's a new doctor in town. I'm sure you're up on all the latest things…"

"But I wouldn't be able to care for him anyway. I'd have to refer you to one of the other veterinarians…"

"Veterinarians?" she screeched.

"Yes. Isn't Max your pet?"

"Max is my *husband*!"

There was a click on the line and I found myself standing there with a dead phone glued to my ear. I looked around at Anton and found him doubled over with laughter.

"You knew she wanted a physician, didn't you" I accused him.

"I thought probably so, but I couldn't resist passing the buck on to you."

I gave him a baleful stare, and putting as much anger in my voice as I could muster, I snarled. "I'll get even with you for this."

We talked Granddad into staying an extra day and going to the reception with us. He agreed and came up with a plan to take us to the dinosaur museum on Thursday afternoon. This area of Alberta is famous for its dinosaur finds. The museum also has specimens of prehistoric animals from other parts of the world. I am not much of a fan of museums, but this one fascinated me once we got there that afternoon.

My favourite display was of an herbivorous dinosaur being attacked by a carnivorous one. The herbivore walked on all fours and its skeleton looked very much like that of a modern large mammal, with the exception that the end of its long tail held a large ball of bone, obviously used for defense. The predatory one was approaching from the flank and its intended prey was looking back over its shoulder. It must have been switching its tail and sending signals that said, "One more step closer Buster and I'll clobber you with my tail!"

"That dino must have had very strong tail muscles to swing that thing around," Anton remarked.

Bird-like creatures, some with huge wingspans, seemed to swoop down from overhead. Leaving the main floor, we went to the area of aquatic exhibits. As we followed the marked path, we noticed that everyone ahead of us seemed to stop suddenly, and then tentatively go on again. When we approached, we did the same thing. It appeared as if we would fall into a deep pool of water if we took a step farther. We then realized that the floor underfoot was Plexiglas and under it was a very realistic display of pre-historic aquatic life. I would have reason to remember this display at a later date.

We stopped at the gift shop and bought T-shirts, postcards and coffee mugs. Granddad also bought mini dinosaurs for his great-grandchildren, the offspring of his two grandsons, my older brother and a cousin.

From the museum, we drove through town and on down the river in order to visit the famous hoodoos. These columns of soil, topped by large flat stones, are the result of many thousands of years of erosion. Wind and rain had washed away the surrounding soil, but under the stones, erosion had not occurred, leaving the columns like statues to the valley's past.

We had dinner at another of the town's restaurants and arrived home in good time to get dressed for the reception.

Earlier that morning I finally met our neighbour, Niall Raymond, who taught computer science. He was still in his bathrobe as he took his garbage out to place his bin beside the street. He was bleary-eyed and crotchety.

"Don't ever knock on my door or phone me before nine o'clock," he grumbled. "I'm not really awake even then. I got the college to agree to giving me only afternoon classes, but they still insist that I be in my office by ten."

I agreed not to disturb him early in the morning, but had my own request of him. "When you come in late at night, would you please refrain from slamming doors. There's not much sound-proofing in these houses, and it wakes us up."

He looked at me for the first time. "Oh, you must be Mrs. Schild."

"I'm Dr. Gail Schild," I snapped back at him. I worked hard for that doctor's degree, and had resolved that I would not allow anyone to call me missus.

"Then you're the genetics prof, not your husband," he exclaimed. "I just assumed it was your husband, because I don't think of women as being profs."

You and I are not going to get along! I thought. "My husband is the professor. I'm a veterinarian. I will be running the emergency clinic." This wasn't exactly true. Anton is a lecturer, not a professor. But I wasn't going to tell that to this jerk.

"Oh, sorry. My mistake. See you around." He stumbled back into his house.

Yes, your mistake Mr. Raymond.

CHAPTER SIX

We were met in the entryway of the president's house by a tubby man with bushy blond hair and a walrus moustache. "I'm Sam Virtue. Come in and meet the Pres. This is Guy Beliveau and his wife Nancie. And you are…?" He used the English pronunciation of the name Guy, not the French one.

"Anton Schild, and this is my wife, Dr. Gail McKinnon. And Gail's grandfather, Gordon McKinnon."

"We are pleased to have you here, Dr. Schild. And Nancie has told me about you, Dr. McKinnon. Welcome to Drayford," the president said. He was a tall man, young looking in spite of his grey hair. Turning to Granddad, he said, "We're glad to have you visit us."

Passing on to Nancie Beliveau, the introductions were repeated.

"I have been wondering where I had seen you before," she said to Granddad, "but now that I've heard your name, I've made the connection. You are Inspector McKinnon who used to lead the RCMP Concert Band, are you not? I remember meeting you at the end of a concert."

Before Granddad could open his mouth to say anything, a young woman who, along with her husband, had preceded us into the room came scurrying over. She gushed an exclamation, "Oh! What are you an inspector of? The Police?"

She was set to continue when, knowing how Granddad hated being called 'inspector,' because he did not want to be constantly explaining that he did not do regular police work, but led the band, I rushed into the breach. "He was Ontario's Apiary Inspector. He inspected all the beehives in the province. We never had a case of foul brood anywhere in the province while he was the inspector. And no one ever got sick from eating Ontario honey. Why, I remember one time…"

Before I could continue, the young woman fled in a panic, a horrified look on her face. Nancie Beliveau had her hands over her mouth to control her mirth. "I'm sorry. I should have realized that you probably didn't want to be referred to that way."

Granddad reassured her. "No harm done. But I'm afraid we've scared that poor young woman."

We wandered into the main room, now filling with people, the sound of polite conversation being punctuated occasionally by a squeal of pleasure as old friends met. There was a bar on one side, and the flow of traffic drifted in that direction. Granddad was swallowed up by a group of the older faculty wives (there were only a few faculty husbands, for the most part looking lost) and I realized that he could take care of himself. We ended up in the company of a middle-aged woman with a sour expression. Anton introduced us. "Professor Hazel Frick, Economics," he said.

"Call me Hazel," she growled. "We are very informal here." Her gaze diverted to the young woman who had accosted Granddad. "Kent Anderson shouldn't have married that silly girl. Look at her, climbing all over him."

"Oh, is that Kent Anderson?" Anton asked. "I want to talk to him." He left me and made his way over to meet the man who might be his rival.

Hazel Frick continued as if she had not noticed Anton's departure. "But then some older men aren't very particular in who they marry, either." I followed her glance toward a morose appearing man of about forty, sitting by himself on a couch at the side of the room, his left arm resting on the armrest, his chin cupped in his hand. "Look at Jon. He says his wife has gone to visit her mother, but I'll bet she's off with a younger man. I can't imagine why he married her."

Looking at her face, I was certain that she was jealous and that she had the hots for the man called Jon. I decided I'd like to meet this man, who seemed lonely, but before I could reach his side of the room, a gawky young woman approached him and spoke. Jon turned his head away, giving her a cold shoulder that should have propelled her into outer space. She seemed indecisive, then eventually walked away. But in the meantime, I wandered over to where Anton was trying to get the attention of Kent Anderson, who was talking to someone else. His young wife turned her attention to the newcomer in their midst. "So you're the guy who makes genetically modified foods," she accused Anton.

"Not food. Grasses," he replied.

"What do you mean grasses plural? There's only one kind of grass. What can you do with grass?"

"You're wrong there. There are many grasses. All the cereal grains are grasses, as is the hay that you feed to your livestock. But the only GM grass I've personally 'made' is ordinary lawn grass."

"So you're making our lawn dangerous to be near."

"Hardly," Anton replied, laughing, which obviously annoyed Mrs. Anderson.

"Don't laugh at me. I know what I'm talking about!"

"No you don't. I helped develop a type of grass that forms a thick matt that holds water in the ground and only grows an inch and a half high, so it never needs to be mowed. That helps the environment because it means you don't have to spew exhaust fumes from your mower into the air, or waste electricity using an electric mower."

"I suppose you make a lot of money making weird things."

"Not a lot. I do share the royalties on the grass. It helped pay my way through school. What's wrong with helping people get something that saves them money and is good for the environment?"

"Oh! I hate you!" She turned her back on Anton, who finally got Kent Anderson's attention.

I made my way over to where the man called Jon was sitting and flopped down on the couch beside him. "I hope you don't mind my sitting here. My feet are killing me." That was true. I'm not used to wearing heels.

"Not at all," he said, proffering his hand to shake mine. "Jon Mendel. I teach math."

So this was the man that Barry at the produce market had told Anton about.

"I understand that you teach an unusual math course."

"That's why I'm here. I'm no farmer. I'm a city boy. When I saw the announcement of this new college, I at first didn't pay much attention. But I did know that most farm families are their own bookkeepers, accountants and financial advisors. They may have someone do their taxes for them, but mostly they handle their finances themselves. So I went to the agriculture faculty at the university where I used to work and got them to give me some examples of the kinds of financial decisions various types of farmers are faced with. Then I made a proposal to Drayford for a course to be taught here, and they liked it, so here I am."

"Can you give me an example?"

"Suppose you are farming a thousand or more acres. You plan to put some of it in canola. What is the best brand of seed to buy? Should you buy equipment or lease it? How many hectares will you put in canola and how many in wheat? Things of that sort."

Anton had wandered over. He now made a comment. "And if your farm happens to be right under a monster thunderstorm and the hail pounds your newly sprouted seedlings back into the ground, it's going to upset all your calculations."

"Yes. So we factor in a contingency plan.

"Take another example. You're a rancher with a cow/calf operation. You want to devise the most economical winter ration for your pregnant cows. First, you have to know the nutritional requirements of your cows. My students go to the animal husbandry department and get information on the optimal nutritional needs. Then they have to get the current cost of each feed that goes into this ration. They then have to juggle things around because some feeds are more expensive than others. Cheapest is almost never the best for the animals, but most expensive will not be affordable. So how much can you reduce an expensive feed and replace it with a cheaper one? When you balance the diet with regard to energy versus protein, will you have a good mineral/vitamin balance, or will you have to add supplements? Will a mineralized salt block provide an adequate mineral ration?

"Once you have decided on the best ration, you also have to factor in the other costs. Fuel for your trucks, insurance, the cost of leasing rangeland. Then you have to study forecasts of likely prices for calves you will sell to determine whether to reduce your herd or add to it.

"The course has become popular with the students because they are mainly farm kids and they have had experience with these problems.

"Of course, there are apps that will do these calculations for you, as Niall Raymond, who teaches computer science, frequently reminds me, but I tell him his apps are for general conditions, not for specific ones. The kids need to be able to decide which one is best, and they need to know the math behind them."

"You sound as if you enjoy teaching this course."

"I do. There are always a few who don't want to do the work, but anyone who does I'll go out of my way to help. The class work isn't all done in the classroom."

"Did you have a good conversation with Kent Anderson?" I asked Anton.

"No. We'll meet some other time. By the way, he's intimidated by you, Dr. Mendel."

"Call me Jon. Kent shouldn't be. He thinks I disapprove of organic farming, but I don't. I just disapprove of some of the airheads that are attracted to his course. They spout slogans, and basically don't know what they're talking about. They say they disapprove of using chemicals and if you say, 'Then you're not going to water your plants' and remind them that water is a chemical, they say, 'You know what I mean.' I tell them that no, I don't know what they mean, and neither do they.

"Kent is trying to use scientific methodology to show the value of organic farming. If he can do it, more power to him."

"That means that if I want to convince you that genetically modified foods are better, I'll have to prove it scientifically."

"That's right."

We talked for a while longer, then as the crowd began to drift toward the door, Jon rose, shook our hands and said, "I enjoyed talking to you. You should come to my house for dinner sometime soon."

Thinking this was merely a courtesy remark, I was about to respond in kind when he went on, "How about Saturday?"

"I can't come Saturday. I agreed to start on September first, which is Friday—tomorrow. I will work five days straight, then have three days off."

"They wouldn't wait and let you start on Tuesday, the day after the Labour Day holiday, eh?"

"The other vets probably wanted one last summer holiday off. I can't blame them. I'll be on duty the next Saturday as well, but the one after that would work out all right."

"Okay. I like to keep weeknights open for students to drop in. Saturday the sixteenth then. I will look forward to seeing you then. Come as soon after five as you can, and bring your swimsuits. We can have a swim before we eat."

As we were getting ready for bed, Anton asked, "What was all that about your granddad inspecting bees? You should have seen the look on his face."

"I know how he hates people like that silly girl asking about his work, so I decided to scare her away. I don't know what made me think of bees, maybe because of your description of that man Barry talking about the separate bee hives. And I can't remember for sure whether fowl brood is a bee disease, but on the spur of the moment it sounded good. And it worked. I do remember once several years ago hearing about some frat boys from some other university, I think it was in the States, finding a beehive in a tree when they were out in the woods and deciding to get the honey and have a party where they made biscuits and served them with butter and honey. One boy got stung so badly, he had to be taken to the hospital, but the others managed to get the honeycombs. They extracted the honey and had their party. Everyone who was there, except the kid with the allergic reaction to the stings, ended up getting violently ill. The public health authorities found an enterotoxin-producing staphylococcus in the honey."

"What were a bunch of frat boys doing out in the woods—studying the birds and the bees?"

"Probably. They had girls with them."

"I seem to remember one fine May day, having the desire to engage in that study, and that we rode our bikes out into the country to do so. But not in the woods."

"No. We did it in a cow pasture."

"Yeah. I recall that the cows wandered over to watch us. They were a bit intimidating."

"I don't remember you being particularly *cowed* by them."

Anton grabbed me, threw me on the bed and dropped down beside me. He murmured into my ear, "Let's study that some more." Which we did, accompanied by laughter and joking.

CHAPTER SEVEN

I arrived at my new clinic a few minutes before seven o'clock on Friday, turned on the lights, switched the phone off of voice mail and checked for messages. There were none. Kevin, the young man who was supposed to work with me showed up at a quarter after seven, accompanied by a girl named Shawna. They said that they had both been hired. I set them to cleaning shelves, which were covered with dust, and arranging the skimpy supply of drugs and supplies. I made a list of supplies I felt I had to have in order to operate the clinic. The workers were slow, and any time my back was turned, they disappeared into the back, where someone had left an old recliner. Kevin was no help at all in restraining the large dog I had to treat.

My first night on the job was a pretty dull one. It would take a while for the word to get around that there was now an emergency clinic open all night. I only had one call, a woman who brought in her black Lab, Duke, with a bleeding foot. It turned out to be only a torn nail, a common problem. We talked as I snipped off the nail, which was hanging by a small piece of skin, cleaned the tender core and placed a sterile dressing on it. I padded it with cotton and bandaged the foot, using lots of tape to keep the bandage from wearing through.

The lady told me she had called Tom Grant, had gotten a voice mail message to call the new clinic. "I'm glad Tom is finally able to take some time off," she said. "He works so hard. This clinic is an excellent idea."

I told her to take Duke to Tom Grant on Monday to have the bandage changed. "It will take some time to grow the new nail and will need to be kept covered until then."

"Can we go out for a coffee?" Shawna asked at about nine o'clock.

"You just got here, and were late at that. You are supposed to take a break at midnight or one o'clock, unless we are busy. There is a lot of cleaning to do in order to get this place in shape. And you need to learn where everything is kept so that when I ask you to get me something, you will know where to find it. You also, I see, need to learn the names of things. When I ask for bandage scissors, I don't want you to bring me surgical scissors. So get to work." She went off pouting.

Around ten o'clock, a scruffy young man, dressed in old jeans and sweatshirt, came in wheeling a fancy blue mountain bike that must have cost over a thousand dollars. I wondered whether he had actually bought the bike or whether he had stolen it. He did not have an animal with him. He was a big guy and with his bike, he filled the tiny waiting room.

"What can I do for you?"

"Is Kevin here?"

"Kevin is working. He can't talk with you now. What do you want with him?"

He gave me a disdainful glance. "You the new vet?"

"Yes. I'm Dr. McKinnon."

"Well tell him Billy was here. I'll see him later on." He wheeled his bike out onto the street and rode away.

A few minutes later, my neighbor, Niall Raymond, dropped in. He was much more lively than he had been early in the morning.

"Just wanted to say hello to you on your first night in your new job." He stayed around for a while, chatting before he eventually wandered off. He appeared perfectly sober but had the smell of liquor on his breath.

The next visitor was in the uniform of the city police. The three chevrons identified him as a sergeant. Of average height and lithe build, he walked with a kind of grace. His ebony skin was as black as a black man could possibly be. He held out his hand saying, "I'm Sgt. Josh Tucker. I like to get acquainted with new businesses in town to see what they need in the way of help from us. Welcome to Drayford, Dr. McKinnon."

We talked for a while. He asked whether I kept any narcotics on the premises.

"Not yet, but I will as soon as I get my authorization to use and to dispense them. They will be kept in a safe." Alex Breling's new Riverside Clinic had given the emergency clinic an old safe salvaged from their previous premises, one that they no longer needed in the new building.

"We keep a close eye on drug stores and medical clinics for any sign of someone trying to break in. I noticed that you don't keep the door locked."

"No."

"I'd suggest that you do after midnight at any rate."

"I'll have a doorbell installed, so people can alert me of their presence if I'm working in the back."

"Do that. And check on what they want before opening the door."

"Okay."

"Do you have anyone working with you?"

"I'm supposed to, but I'm probably going to fire the ones who are here tonight," I growled.

"Well, we're just a phone call away if you need us."

I was to get to know Sgt. Tucker very well in the near future.

When Tucker had left, I told my helpers that I was going to step across the street to the Tim Hortons, which was open all night, for a coffee. I asked them whether they wanted me to bring them anything, thinking I could treat them as a good-will gesture. "No thanks," they told me. I locked the door behind me. When I returned ten minutes later, they were gone. They did not return at any time that night.

The next day, they were half an hour late. And when business was slow later in the evening, they suggested to me, "Why don't you go home? There's nothing to do."

I knew they wanted me to leave so that they could skip out again. I reminded them that we were all supposed to be working throughout the night. I vowed that I would talk to Alex Breling the first thing Tuesday morning, when he came back from his holiday weekend, about the employee situation. I needed reliable help.

That night, I had three cases. Two of them I treated and sent home, but I had to keep the other one, which came in shortly before midnight, overnight. I started an IV, and my two helpers were told to keep an eye on the dog to prevent it getting the IV line kinked or pulled out. I had bought a camp cot, which I set up in my office, and at about two in the morning, I lay down for a nap, telling the kids to watch the dog while I was asleep. Not completely trusting them, I woke up about an hour later and checked my patient. The dog had pulled out the IV catheter and the fluid which was supposed to be dripping into its vein had all run out onto the bottom of the cage, which was now soggy. At least the dog was feeling much better, standing up and wagging its tail. I went to find my helpers with murder, or at least mayhem, in my mind. They were sound asleep. Shawna was sitting on Kevin's lap in the old recliner.

When I managed to wake them up, I realized that both were stoned. I remembered that I heard them talking to someone earlier in the evening when I was in the exam room treating one of the cases. When I went back into the waiting room, after finishing with the patient, I saw Billy riding away on his fancy blue mountain bike, saddlebags slung across the rear wheel. My helpers had not shown any signs of drug use earlier in the evening, so they must have taken the drugs while I was napping. I fired them on the spot, and sent them home. I would have to run the clinic single-handed until I could find someone to replace them, but I couldn't possibly use anyone who could not be counted on to remain lucid during the time they were at work.

In the morning, I called the Donaldsons at home and they came in their Mercedes SUV to pick up the dog and transfer it to their clinic for further treatment. I was to find that I could count on the Donaldsons and on Tom Grant to pick up their patients by my seven AM closing time, but the Riverside Clinic and Irwin Prouse might turn up at any time in the morning to collect animals their answering services had referred to me. This became one of the ongoing problems I had to face.

When I left that morning and was locking the door, a cruising cop car came by and I flagged it down. I told the policeman that I thought that the man I knew only as Billy was probably a drug dealer and was using my clinic as a drop-off point. I felt certain that Kevin and Shawna had gotten their drugs from him, and suspected that was why Niall Raymond had come to my clinic. Niall had dropped by again that night, talked for a while, then left. I thought he had been using some drug, probably a street drug. The policeman told me that they had their eye on Billy, but as yet had not been able to find him with drugs in his possession.

When Billy learned that Kevin no longer worked there, he no longer dropped into the clinic.

Sunday night another of the town's vets dropped by.

"Hi! I'm Jim Dunn. My partner and I do the farm animal work. He does cattle and I do horses. I rarely have a small animal case except when I'm out on a farm, but occasionally I have to refer someone to one of you small animal vets. I thought I'd drop by and say hello."

"I'm glad to meet you, Jim. I've had one query about a horse, but I told the people to call you. We don't keep any equine meds here."

"Right. By the way, don't you have anyone here to help you?"

I told him about my employee problems and that I planned to advertise for replacements. His response to that was a welcome reminder that there are good people in this world.

"Look. If you need any help in the next day or two, give me a call. I can assist with surgery or give anesthetics while you do surgery. Like if you have to do a Caesarian, you need people to take care of the pups or kittens while you finish closing up the mom. My wife and kids would be willing to come help with that. I mean it. Call me."

I got to know Jim Dunn well over the next few months and always found him pleasant and helpful.

The next week I advertised for replacement helpers, and got an eager response from half a dozen applicants. So much for Alex Breling's complaint that I should not have fired what he called 'experienced workers.'

I hired a woman who had been a receptionist for a veterinary clinic in Calgary before her husband had been transferred to Drayford. Gerry would work from seven to ten in the evening, and from six to nine in the morning on the nights I was on call. Her husband would be home on the evenings she worked and her two teenagers could get themselves off to school in the mornings.

Samantha (call me Sam) was a student at the college, but was willing to do nighttime work and take afternoon classes. She turned out to be excellent with both dogs and cats, and willing to take time to make them comfortable. She would work a ten-hour shift on the five nights I was at the clinic. The other vets agreed to provide their own helpers on the nights they were on call. My work settled into a comfortable routine.

CHAPTER EIGHT

We arrived at Jon's house a little after five on Saturday the sixteenth. Jon was already in swim trunks and showed us to the bedroom where we could change into ours. We joined him in the pool, a welcome place to be on this late summer day. There was a roof over the pool, and removable walls, so that it could be an outdoor pool in the summertime, but an indoor one during cooler seasons. I suspected that Jon swam year round.

"I always have my handyman come on September fifteenth to put up the walls. This year, it's still been hot during the day and I wish the pool were still open, but the guy has a busy schedule and I didn't want to have to reschedule," Jon explained.

We swam for about half an hour, lay around for a while drying off with soft luxurious bath towels, then returned to the bedroom to change back into our clothes. As Anton picked up his pants, coins spilled out of a pocket and dropped into the deep pile of the dark brown carpet. We scrambled around trying to find the coins, most of which had disappeared. I didn't want to leave any for a vacuum cleaner to run over. I piled them on the bedside table. Anton remarked, as he stuffed coins back into his pocket, that it was as well that Canada no longer used pennies. They would be hard to find in this carpet.

I joined Jon in his well-appointed kitchen. There was an appetizing aroma emanating from the oven, and Jon was chopping ingredients for a salad, using a knife from a beautiful set with his and his wife's initials engraved in the handles.

"Several of our friends together gave us this set as a wedding present. It is top quality German steel, and it holds its edge much better than ordinary knives. Leah and I both enjoy cooking, so you will have to come again some time after she returns."

While I was talking to Jon in the kitchen, Anton was wandering around the dining room looking at paintings in a style that seemed to be a cross between landscape and hologram. Wild animals seemed to appear out of the forest and sink back into it, depending on the angle at which you viewed the painting. "Fascinating!" he exclaimed.

"Those are Leah's. She is very talented." There was a tone of profound admiration in his voice. Whenever he spoke of his wife, it was with loving tenderness. I thought to myself that the economics prof, Hazel Frick, hadn't a chance with him and knew it, which is probably what caused her to be catty about his wife. I had heard other remarks around campus to the effect that Leah Mendel was overly friendly with Niall Raymond. I wondered how accurate they were. Jon never mentioned a reason for Leah's absence. Could there be anything to the rumours? I hoped not.

After a dinner of roast lamb accompanied by an excellent Okanagan Valley wine, followed by coffee made the old fashioned way with an electric percolator, we went into the living room and Jon placed a CD in the player. "This is

Rodrigo's Concerto de Aranjuez with Pepe Romero and Neville Mariner. I love this recording. It was made under the direct supervision of Rodrigo himself." He gave us a knowledgeable account of each record he played. He was obviously well versed on the subject of classical music. At one time the doorbell rang and his discussion of the music was interrupted by his going to the door. The visitor was Niall Raymond, I didn't see him but recognized his voice, and Jon called him Niall.

"I didn't realize you had company," I heard Niall say. "I'll come back later."

While the music played we conversed on a number of subjects, from politics to sport. He had definite opinions on some of the issues we discussed, but was willing to listen to other opinions and to give serious attention to them. Time flew by as we delved into many subjects ranging from how the justices of the Supreme Court of Canada were chosen to whether children should be required to be vaccinated before entering school. He also was knowledgeable about local history, though he had only lived here for a little over two years.

"The town got its name because there is a shallow part of the river, with a rocky bottom, about a kilometer downstream. In the late summer and early fall, it was possible to drive teams of horses pulling those big freight wagons called drays, across the river at that ford. At other times of year, they had to pull barges across the river with teams of horses on the banks of the river. Eventually a ferry was built, but in the nineteen fifties the first bridge was built."

Finally, Anton looked at his watch and exclaimed, "It's past ten thirty. I'd lost track of time because you are such an interesting person to talk to, Jon, but I think it's time Gail and I took our leave."

"I have enjoyed it myself," Jon replied. "We must get together again. Leah will be back next month and you must meet her."

He escorted us to the door and stepped out onto the small porch to bid us goodbye. As we went down the walk to the street, a neighbor, having trouble controlling his rambunctious dog, waved a greeting to Jon and joined us as we walked.

"Lovely night, isn't it?" he remarked. We ambled along together as far as the college gate, at which point he bid us goodnight and turned back.

The night was still warm. We stopped at the Dragon Fountain, at night lit by red and gold lights making the drops of water sparkle as they fell. As we watched the light show, Anton said, "I haven't enjoyed a discussion like that in ages. We could debate all the pros and cons of a contentious subject without arguing and without anyone trying to make everyone else accept their opinion. I really enjoyed it."

"I agree. I think we have found a real friend."

It was somewhere around midnight when we went to bed, and in that half-life between consciousness and sleep, I heard our neighbor, Niall, come home. He banged the door, which he still occasionally did in spite of his promise. I heard him moving about, and then heard another sound, which I identified as that of a normal household appliance. I remember thinking that the sound insulation in these houses was decidedly inadequate and that on the night of the president's reception Niall must have gotten an earful of our antics in the bedroom. Perhaps we should move to the other bedroom, where a large closet was located between the room and the dividing wall. With that, I fell asleep.

CHAPTER NINE

Anton again, taking up the narrative. Gail was still asleep when, at five in the morning, I got up to go on my early morning run around the campus, so I'll tell this part of the story.

Mornings were crisp and I debated about whether to wear a jacket. I decided not. I would soon warm up and have to take it off and it would then become a nuisance. I started off at a brisk pace, heading for the Ad building to get a cup of coffee from the janitors. After that I ran around the gym and playing fields at the far end of the campus and back around the upper side of the loop. None of the shopkeepers were out yet so I went on toward the Dragon Fountain.

I was surprised to see two police cars parked beside the fountain and cops talking to the maintenance workers. I stopped to see what was going on. One of the policemen, a very black man wearing sergeant's chevrons, was directing another cop who was delicately climbing into the pool, now dry, and reaching into a crevice under the foot of a dragon. He tied a piece of string around an object that was lying there and gently worked it free. Holding it aloft by the string, he made his way back out of the fountain and handed the object he had retrieved to the sergeant. It was a knife, a long, slender one with a narrow blade and engraving on the handle. At the place where the blade joined the handle, dark red clots could be seen. The policemen gathered around to look closely.

"Looks like blood," one of the cops remarked.

"Yeah," the sergeant replied. "It was in the water, but under that dragon's foot, the water was stagnant, so any blood on the blade would have been washed off, but the clots there near the handle weren't."

"I know where that knife comes from!" I exclaimed.

The sergeant whirled toward me and asked, "Who are you?"

"Anton Schild. I'm a lecturer at the college."

"What do you know about this knife?"

"I recognize it as being one from a set. Those are the owners' initials engraved in the handle."

"And what do you know about it being in the basin of the fountain?"

"All I know is that it wasn't here last night."

"Where was it?"

"I'd better explain. Last night, my wife and I were guests of Dr. Jon Mendel, a math professor here at the college. We had dinner there, and were in the kitchen watching him work. My wife commented on the knife set, and Jon told us it had been given to him and his wife as a wedding present."

"Was he using this knife?"

"No. This is a filet knife. He was using another one from the set to chop vegetables."

"You say it was a set. Were the knives in a holder?"

"Yes, they were."

"Are you sure this knife was there?"

"Yes, it was."

"What time was that?"

"We left the house a little after ten-thirty."

"Were there any other guests?"

"No."

"Did anyone else see you leave the house?"

"Yes. A neighbour who was walking his dog joined us and walked as far as the college gate with us." I realized, with a jolt to my stomach, that Gail and I were being considered as prime suspects in anything that might have happened in Jon's house after we left. I hastened to add, "He waved to Jon, who had seen us to the door, and Jon waved back."

"We'll check on that. I think we'd better go to Dr. Mendel's house. Can you show us where he lives?"

"Yes. It's not far from here."

He opened the back door of one of the police cars and motioned for me to climb in. Before he got into the car, he asked the maintenance workers to keep the water for the fountain turned off until further notice. The chief of the crew said he would do so and I saw the workers resume their job of removing coins from the pool.

At the house, the sergeant let me out and took my arm to escort me to the door. When there was no answer to his ring, he directed one of his minions to try the door. It was locked.

"Let's go around to the back."

There was a back door into the kitchen, also locked, so we went on around to the door leading to the pool, the sergeant still clutching my arm. I noticed that the lights around the pool were still on. A policeman tried the door and found it unlocked.

"Go in," the sergeant said, "and take a look around."

It did not take the man long, and when he came out, I could see by the look on his face that I'd better be prepared for what I would see when we entered the pool enclosure.

The first thing I noticed when we entered was the water in the pool. Normally it reflected the blue of the tile lining the pool. Now it was red! I stepped forward and looked into the pool. Jon Mendel was lying face down on the bottom.

The sergeant, still holding my arm moved slowly up the side of the pool until we reached an area covered with splatters of blood. He held me back. "Don't step on any of that," he commanded. I looked again into the pool. No blood was issuing from any part of Jon's body, and I couldn't tell where the blood that was staining the pool had come from.

"We'll have to get him out of the pool," the sergeant said. "How are we going to do that?"

None of the cops seemed eager to go into the water so I offered. "Look, I'm only wearing shorts and a T-shirt. I can go into the pool and pull him out better than any of you can. I can get my wife to bring me some dry clothes."

He considered for a moment then agreed. "Go up to the shallow end, but go around the pool on the other side so you don't walk across this area where the blood is."

I walked around the pool, took off my shoes and socks, and waded into the shallow end before diving down to the body. Grasping it by an arm, I surfaced and kicked my way along to where I could stand up. I'm pretty strong, as a result of growing up on a farm, where one of my chores was stacking bales of hay. I lifted John's body and carried it up the steps, laying it down on the edge of the pool. I noticed that rigor was starting in the neck and shoulders but was not well established, so that when I lifted the body free of the water, the head lolled back a bit, and a great glob of bloody water welled up out of the severed trachea. I could see the severed blood vessels on both sides of the neck, now emptied of blood. I had to fight down a wave of nausea. I staggered over to a rack where towels were hung and dried my face and hair.

"Well, that explains where the blood came from," the sergeant commented.

"I'd like to call my wife and have her bring me some dry clothes if that's all right with you." I was shivering as I removed my T-shirt and wrung it out.

"I guess that's all right. She's Dr. McKinnon, isn't she?"

"Yes."

"I've met her at her clinic. I'll need to talk to her about last night anyway. I don't want you using the house phone here, but I'll dial her number on my phone."

I gave him our home phone number, he dialed, waited for the ring tone and handed his phone to me. I asked Gail, who sounded sleepy, to bring me a dry shirt and pair of shorts. "How come your clothes are wet?" she asked, now sounding more alert. "Where are you?"

"At Jon's."

I heard her bite back a comment, as she must have heard something in my voice that said the request was serious. "I'll be right over."

CHAPTER TEN

When Anton called me, I was about to make some flippant remark about falling into a pool of water in the middle of a desert, but caught a tone of anxiety in his voice that made me think something serious had happened. I pulled on some clothes, grabbed a pair of shorts and a T-shirt for Anton and jumped into the car. I might as well have walked. There was no place to park anywhere near Jon's house. The street seemed filled with police cars, an ambulance, and an assortment of neighbour's vehicles. I parked several houses away and ran back to Jon's. A constable guarding the front door directed me around to the back once he had established my identity.

I was allowed to enter the pool enclosure and was struck by the tense poses of everyone there. There were policemen staring at the floor at the edge of the pool about half way down without getting near the object of their attention. At the far end, Anton was standing near someone who was lying on the floor. I followed his gaze toward the pool. Red! Why was the water red?

I recognized Sgt. Tucker, who motioned me to come around the pool on the side opposite the one where the other cops were standing. As I reached the far end of the pool, I recognized the recumbent man as Jon, wearing his swimsuit. A second glance showed me the severed vessels in his neck. I felt suddenly weak and Anton caught me by the arm to steady me.

I quietly handed Anton his dry clothes. He stepped out of his wet shorts and pulled on the dry ones. I noticed that I had grabbed the Guelph Gryphons T-shirt. Oh well. Who cared right now? From this end of the pool I could see that the cops on the side of the pool were interested in an area of blood splatters. I moved closer, but Tucker held me back.

"Was his body in the pool?" I asked. Anton nodded, and Tucker asked, "Why do you ask that?"

I leaned over Jon's body and pointed to a dark red spot on his abdominal wall, just below the rib cage. "He was stabbed there first," I said.

"What makes you think that?"

"He must have been standing when he was stabbed there. It would be hard to stab a person in the abdomen if he was in the pool and you were leaning over from the side of the pool."

"The person who stabbed him could have been swimming with him."

"Carrying a knife?"

Tucker laughed at that. "Maybe."

"But he wasn't. He was standing on the edge, and he was wearing hard-soled shoes. Look at Jon's fingers." I pointed to the fingers of Jon's left hand. They were crushed, with broken skin and obvious fractures. I reached for the right hand, but Tucker grabbed my hand and demanded, "Don't touch the body."

Anton was standing on the other side of Jon's body. He bent over for a look. "The index finger on his right hand is smashed also."

I went on, "When he was stabbed, he must have fallen into the pool, then tried to grab the side and pull himself out. Then his assailant stepped on his fingers and ground them into the tiles, then leaned over and slashed his throat."

"Maybe the slash to the throat made him fall into the pool."

I shook my head. "Once that happened, he didn't do anything."

"Why do you say that?"

"Because it would only take one or two heart beats to empty enough blood out of his body for his blood pressure to drop precipitously. Besides, he would not have any blood going to his brain. He might have inhaled a lungful of water with one breath after he was slashed, but he wasn't doing anything else."

Tucker looked at me with an ominous frown on his face. "You seem to know a lot about it."

"Well, it's obvious. I know enough physiology to figure that out." My voice got more aggressive as I spoke. It had suddenly occurred to me that Anton and I, being the last people to see Jon, were the logical suspects. I'd better fight fire with fire. "But don't take my word for it. Your medical examiner will tell you the same thing. And your forensic team will be able to tell by the blood splatters where he was when his throat was slashed. The other stab wound wouldn't have splashed blood, but the throat certainly would."

I turned to Anton. "How come you're here?"

"I jogged past the Dragon Fountain and saw the police there. I went over to see what was going on and saw that they'd found a knife with blood on it in the fountain. I recognized the knife as one from the set Jon had been showing us last night, and the sergeant hasn't let me out of his sight since. We came over here and found Jon's body in the bottom of the pool."

"You must have gone into this pool to get the body out."

Anton nodded.

Tucker wanted to know, "How come you know so much about these knives?"

"Jon was really proud of them. He said they were very well made German knives that hold their edge better than most. They were given to the Mendels as a wedding present."

"You looked at them. Did you handle any of them?"

"Yes. He was using one, but he pulled another out of the rack to show me."

"Which one?"

"I think it was a filet knife." I realized right away, from Anton's sudden inhalation of breath, that I had just told the policeman that I had handled the murder weapon. My fingerprints must be all over it. I added weakly, "I'm not sure though."

CHAPTER ELEVEN

The forensic technicians had arrived on the scene while Tucker was talking to me. He excused himself for a moment to speak to them. When he came back, he instructed one of his cops to take us into the living room. "Take a seat there and I'll be in to talk to you in a few minutes. Don't touch anything, and don't talk to each other."

It was rather boring, being told not to do anything, and time seemed to drag. It must have been half an hour before Tucker arrived to relieve his man, who nevertheless remained in the room. "Now, let's go over the events of last night. What time did you get here for your visit?"

Anton took the lead in answering Tucker's questions. "A little after five. I came directly from work and met Gail here. She brought me my swimsuit." I nodded my agreement.

"Did you go swimming first, before supper?"

"Yes."

"Did Dr. Mendel go swimming also, or was he busy cooking supper?"

"He went swimming. He had a roast in the oven, and prepared the rest of the meal after our swim."

"Were you in the kitchen all the time while he was doing so?"

"Gail was, mostly." Anton looked at me for confirmation. I nodded.

"And what were you doing?"

"I was looking at the paintings. They're by Leah, Jon's wife. The technique is fascinating."

"What do you mean?"

"Just look at them." Anton waved toward the ones displayed in the living room. Tucker got up to have a look and came back with a pleased expression. "I see what you mean. Was Leah Mendel here?"

"No. He said she was away for the rest of the month."

"Where? Do you know?"

"No. He didn't say."

Tucker turned toward me. "Were you helping Dr. Mendel?"

"No. He seemed to be a very self-sufficient sort of person."

"But you were handling the knives."

"One knife. I had noticed how attractive the handles were. He pulled one out to show me the engraving in the handle."

"But he gave it to you?"

"He handed it to me, butt first, very carefully. He made sure I had a good grip on it before he let go."

"Did you hold it in both hands?"

"Yes, I did. I turned it over to get a good look at it."

Tucker turned to the constable who had been waiting in the background. "Go get Coté. We will need to get Dr. McKinnon's fingerprints." While we waited, Tucker said, "We checked the knives in the rack and one is missing. It seems pretty definite that the weapon was one from that set."

59

In a few minutes, one of the members of the forensic team entered the room, fingerprint kit in hand, and took my prints.

"I think we might as well take Dr. Schild's while we're at it. And while you're here, dust the phone and see what prints you can pick up. It has rung a couple of times and I haven't answered it. It displays the number that is calling, but I recognized who made those calls and I don't want to talk to the press yet. But I might want to use that phone myself."

The phone yielded a fine crop of prints, and Coté remarked, "I can tell you right now that all those prints were made by the victim. I just took his prints and I recognize these."

"Thanks. That's what I expected. What about the knife?"

"It had been wiped clean. There wasn't a print on it. But when the blade was wiped off, it was probably done hastily and missed the blood up where the blade fits into the handle."

"Thanks."

But Coté seemed puzzled. "Why the hell did the guy take the knife with him? Why not just throw it in the pool?"

Tucker shrugged. "People in a panic do strange things sometimes. Maybe he didn't realize he still had the knife in his hand until he had run away, and then was too scared to go back."

Tucker settled back in his chair as if to make himself comfortable for a long session, so I decided that two could play this game. I shoved a cushion into the corner of the couch and nestled into it. If he was going to keep us here for a while, I was going to show him that I intended to be comfortable. Anton remained in his armchair. I could sense an alertness in his attitude.

But before Tucker could get started, the phone rang. He indicated that his constable should answer it. After a brief exchange, the constable handed the phone to Tucker. "A prof named Hazel Frick. She lives nearby and wants to know what's going on here."

Tucker took the phone and after listening to the caller, said, "We aren't making a statement yet. We are still investigating. All I can tell you now is that Dr. Mendel is deceased, under suspicious circumstances. If you know anything about him, we would like to talk to you." He took her address and said he would come to talk to her later that morning. "Please remain at home until we come."

He resumed his seat but appeared less relaxed. "Were there any other guests at this dinner party?" He asked it of me. Anton told me later that Tucker had already asked him that. I thought it must have been an attempt to see whether we gave conflicting testimony.

"No."

"So no one else was there?"

"Someone came to the door, but didn't come in."

"Who was it?"

"I didn't see him, but Jon called him 'Niall' so I assume that it was Niall Raymond."

"Do you know Mr. Raymond?"

"Yes. He's our neighbour in faculty housing."

"Did he say anything to Dr. Mendel?"

"When John told him he had company, Niall said he would come back later."

"What time later, did he say?"

"No. I think it was just a commonplace kind of remark."

"No other conversation?"

"I think he asked if Leah was there."

"Leah is Dr. Mendel's wife?"

"Yes."

"What did Dr. Mendel say?"

"He said that she was away."

"Anything else?"

"No."

"You're sure?"

"Yes."

"Any other callers?"

"No."

Tucker glanced at Anton. "How about you? Can you remember any other visitors?"

"No."

Back to me. "What time did you leave?"

"About a quarter to eleven, I think."

"Did you see anyone else on your way home?"

"There was a man walking his dog. We talked for a while and he went with us as far as the gate." I saw Anton relax slightly and saw the constable in the background note Anton's reaction.

"Did you walk home?"

"Yes. We stopped to admire the fountain. It's beautiful at night."

"Did you go directly home from there?"

"Yes. And we then went directly to bed."

"Did you see Mr. Raymond?"

"No." Should I tell Tucker that I heard Raymond come in later? I decided not to unless asked.

The constable said to Tucker, "I saw Raymond downtown later in the evening."

"What time?"

"I went on duty at eleven, so some time after about eleven thirty. He's a regular in this town's night scene, so I didn't particularly notice the exact time. But I know he was there."

"I can verify that he's a regular in the night scene," I remarked. "He frequently drops by my clinic."

Tucker nodded. "Okay. I've talked to the neighbour and he has verified your account. He also said Dr. Mendel came to the door to see you off. So you are free to go. I may have more questions later, but that's it for now."

As we stepped out the door, the young woman who had tried to talk to Jon at the president's reception came bursting up the steps.

"Oh, don't tell me it's true. Is Jon dead?" she wailed.

"Who are you?" Tucker asked.

"I'm Patty Nelson. Is Jon dead?"

"Are you a student here?"

"I'm not a student," she said as if the question were insulting. "I'm assistant manager of the college stables."

"Stables? As in horses?"

"Yeah, that what a stable is."

"Don't get hot under the collar. I'm just trying to get information. Where do you live?"

"I have an apartment at the stables. I live there."

"Okay. Go home. Calm yourself down, and I'll come up to see you later."

"But I want to know…" Tucker shut the door in her face.

"Poor girl," I said quietly to Anton as we made our way down the front walk. "Nobody takes her seriously."

"Yeah. But you notice, all the wannabe girlfriends are showing up."

We walked to where I had left the car and I remarked to Anton. "He asked you those questions before I came, didn't he?"

"Yes, he did. He must have wanted to see if we told a consistent story. That's the advantage in telling the truth in the first place. I'm sure he wanted to trip us up. But I don't think we're off the hook. I think he's just giving us some rope."

"If so, we'd better be sure to keep our noses clean."

My granddad would have approved of that sentiment. When we got home, my cell phone, which I hadn't taken with me in my haste, was ringing. Inspector Gordon McKinnon, in all his professional pomposity, was on the line.

"I've been worried about you Gail. I heard that you and Anton were involved in a murder and were being interrogated by the police. I do hope you haven't told them anything or signed any statement."

"Granddad, whatever made you think I was 'involved' in a murder?"

"I heard that a professor was murdered. That is true, isn't it?"

"It is true, yes. But we aren't 'involved.' How did you hear about it so soon?"

"A lady I met at your president's reception sent me an e-mail and I've been trying to get hold of you ever since."

"Well, tell your lady friend to get her facts straight before she goes around spreading wild rumours." I was getting angry. "Anton and I are among dozens of people who have been, or will be questioned about the man who died. That does not mean that any of us is a murderer."

"Gail, take some advice from me. You have to be careful what you say, and it is best not to say anything. I've heard several of my colleagues in the RCMP say that most people who are suspected of a crime talk too much and can talk themselves into being arrested by the police. You need a lawyer before you say anything, and he can tell you what to talk about and what not to."

"Gramps, I thought you didn't want to be considered a part of the police."

"But it's different when it's my granddaughter's freedom is at stake."

"My freedom isn't at stake."

"That's what you may think. I'm going to come out there. And I'm going to get you a lawyer."

"Please don't! If you do, everyone will think we have something to hide, and we don't."

"I'll be there tomorrow morning." Before I could say anything more, the line went dead.

"What on earth was that about?" Anton asked.

"Inspector McKinnon is rushing to my rescue from the evil forces of the police. He apparently has a girl friend here who sends him e-mails and has told him that we've been interrogated by the cops."

"Oh God! He'll probably call your parents also. Maybe you'd better call them first."

But when I called home, I got their voice mail telling me they were vacationing in Mexico and couldn't be reached until they came home.

CHAPTER TWELVE

That afternoon I ran into Hazel Frick in the supermarket. She brought her black cloud along with her. She progressed down the aisle like a steamroller. When she bumped into a young woman wheeling a cart, a baby strapped into its seat, and holding the hand of a small girl who was trying to get loose, Hazel gave the young woman an angry glare and continued her progress. She picked up a package of meat, inspected it and threw it back. I decided to do my shopping in another area of the store. I didn't get away from her, however. She ended up in the checkout line just behind me. The store was crammed with Sunday shoppers, so the line moved slowly. I was stuck.

If Hazel was looking for a place to unload her grievances, she had found it.

"That black policeman came to my house and questioned me as if I were a common criminal. I didn't think a black man could get so high up in the police. They should send for someone from Calgary to take over."

"They are only trying to find out all they can about Jon's life. They will talk to everyone who knew him. It doesn't mean they suspect you."

"I don't think they know what they're doing."

"They seem very competent. I've seen them work, and I think they are going about it in a thorough and orderly fashion. I have confidence in them." Did I? What do I know about police work?

Hazel looked at me as if seeing me for the first time. "Oh, that's right. You're Anton Schild's wife aren't you?"

"I am."

"What were you doing there? I saw you come out of Jon's house this morning."

"We had dinner with Jon last night, so we are apparently the last people besides the person who killed him to see him alive. We're probably prime suspects ourselves because of that, so don't think they are targeting you."

"Humph! So you had dinner with him. I suppose you went swimming, too."

"We did."

"I don't suppose his wife was there."

"She is away."

"If she'd been there, I don't think you'd have been invited. He might have invited your husband, but that wife of his would be sure he didn't invite any other young women. She wouldn't be able to stand up to the competition."

I couldn't help rubbing it in. "She needn't have worried. He was obviously deeply in love with her."

"He'd soon find out. She wouldn't have lasted long."

I thought I'd better not say it…but I did. "You really should withdraw your claws." Hazel didn't seem to hear me though, and I found myself at the head of the line and able to get away once I paid for my purchases. I fled to my car and hurried away before she could catch up with me again. As I drove home, I fleetingly wondered whether Hazel Frick was considered by the police to be a viable suspect in Jon Mendel's murder.

On my way home I detoured up to the college markets to get some veggies. We bought our staples at the supermarket, but got our fresh stuff from the college farm. I had to wait for a woman who was arguing about the price of melons with a student who was working at the shop. I placed her as the wife of the college treasurer, Sam Virtue. At least she had been with him at the president's reception. So this was the woman who thought I should skip work to attend a faculty wives meeting! When she had finished her argument with the student, she turned toward me.

"You're Mrs. Shields, aren't you?"

"I'm Dr. Gail Schild."

"Well, Mrs. Shields, we are disappointed that you did not chose to honour us with your presence at our last meeting. We expect to see you at our next one, Tuesday at Anna Hopkins' home. Bring a salad or a vegetable dish."

"I won't be there. I work nights. And I'm not a faculty wife. I'm the veterinarian who operates the emergency clinic."

"You weren't working last night. You were having dinner at Jon Mendel's house."

"I do take the occasional night off, but Tuesday is not one of them. And I'm not in the least interested in your group."

"What do you know about this murder? I hear that the police are interviewing lots of people. I don't know why they haven't come to see me. I could give them a lot of useful information."

"What do you know about Jon's death?" I wondered if she really did know anything or was just looking for attention and feeling left out.

"I don't know anything about his murder, but I know a lot about his wife. That marriage wouldn't have lasted. That girl flirts with every man on the campus, including the married ones. You should have seen her the other day…"

I made my escape in the middle of her tirade.

Anton had a conversation with Jon's other wannabe girlfriend. I had regaled him with my views on Hazel Frick and Della Virtue, so he described his encounter with Patty Nelson when he came home later in the afternoon. He went to the gym to try to unwind from his stressful morning with a handball game. On the way home, he stopped at the dairy bar to get milk and ice cream. Patty Nelson was there.

"That guy, Sgt. Tucker I think his name is, came around to see me and basically accused me of killing Jon."

Another potential suspect venting her anger at being questioned. At least she didn't say anything about Tucker's skin colour. Anton thought that she seemed more upset by his questions about her relationship with Jon than she was about being considered a suspect. She must be aware that there was comment among the faculty and staff, and probably the students, about her crush on the math professor. I wondered whether there were other women pining over his death. He didn't seem like the kind of man who would have the girls falling at his feet. But the next suspect to express his anger was a man.

CHAPTER THIRTEEN

I did not have an afternoon nap, so I hoped I'd be busy way into the night. It is easier to stay awake when you're busy. I had my camp cot to sack out on if I needed to, but I generally let Sam, my new technician, have it. When I went home the next morning, I could sleep all day if I wanted, but she had to be ready for classes in the afternoon.

My first case was waiting for me when I arrived. The owner was both tired from a long drive to and from Calgary to attend a funeral, and grumpy because his dog, which he had left overnight at a boarding kennel, was coughing when he picked it up. It was a typical case of kennel cough, caused by a virus, but sometimes made worse by a bacterial infection. Like colds in humans, there is no magic medicine to get the dog over it, but neither is it a serious condition. The man complained about the kennel, but I told him that if the dog had only been there for one day, it had been incubating the disease before it went to the kennel.

"And I just got the kennel cough vaccine. How come he still came down with the disease?"

"It takes about two weeks after the vaccine is given for full immunity to develop," I explained.

When he left, I called the kennel. "I just treated a dog that was boarding at your place last night. It has kennel cough, so I thought you ought to know."

"Yeah, I know. I noticed it last night, after the owner left. So I put the dog in another room where there were no other dogs. As a matter of fact, I put it in the cat room. He's a quiet dog, so he wouldn't upset the cats too much. And we handled him last and walked him by himself. Also the kids scrubbed their hands after handling him."

"Good. I assured the guy that his dog didn't pick it up at your kennel."

"Thanks."

The next case was a dog with a cheat grass awn in its ear, a very common complaint in this part of the country in the late summer and fall, when the wild grass is dry. Using an otoscope, I reached into the ear with alligator forceps and plucked out the offending awn.

While working on this dog, Niall Raymond wandered in. He sat patiently until the client left with his dog. He wanted to talk. He restlessly paced the waiting room floor while he poured out his troubles. He had been drinking—I could smell it on his breath—but he was not drunk. I had come to realize that Niall could imbibe enough liquor to put the average person under the table, but still not show any signs. He was another one who thought the cops were singling him out as suspect number one. "They were at me all day; where was I every minute of last night, what was I doing, why did I go to Jon's that late in the evening, how well did I know Jon. All kinds of stuff."

"Why *did* you go to Jon's last night?"

"Now, don't you start on me. I went there because Jon and I are friends. We argue a lot, but we're friends. And it wasn't late in the evening. I consider nine o'clock to be early."

"What did you argue about?"

"Oh, whether you need to know all that stuff Jon taught when you can use an app to get it a lot quicker."

I refrained from telling him why Jon thought his students needed to know the background and not to rely completely on an app to give them their answers, because I'm sure Jon had tried to drive that into Niall's head himself.

"Last night, I had a new one I wanted to show Jon. It solves some of the problems Jon claimed made the older ones not so good. This new one does everything."

"You said you'd be back later…"

"How'd you know that?"

"I was there, remember. I heard you talking to Jon. When were you going to come back?"

"Hey, you're as bad as that cop. Gimme a break? What does it matter when I was coming back? What I said was just an expression people use."

"Actually I told Sgt. Tucker that. That was the impression I had."

"Well, sorry. I'm sorry I'm so short-tempered tonight, but it's no fun being accused of murder."

"I know. We're on Tucker's list too."

"Oh, yeah. You would be. You were with him last night. How'd he seem. Was he worried about anything?"

"He didn't seem to be, but then we only just met Jon, so we don't know much about him."

"He was a good guy, you know."

"Yes, we know."

Word had gotten around that there was now a veterinary clinic open at night. Some of my clients these days were people who worked nine to five jobs and were willing to pay the higher emergency call fee rather than taking time off work to take their pet to the vet. I didn't give routine vaccinations or do non-emergency surgery. But even without those, I was getting busy in the early evening. When Sgt. Tucker came by, he had to wait while I saw a couple of cases. Both were cats with abscesses caused by bites from another cat, a very common complaint. I wondered whether the cats had been fighting each other, but that thought was squelched when I found that the owners lived on opposite sides of town. When I had time, I took Tucker into my office and told him I was ready for the inquisition. He laughed at that. Some people say that cops have no sense of humour and don't like jokes, and I can see the reason for that, but Tucker seemed to be an exception. Still, he had some serious questions to ask.

"We are wondering whether the back door into the pool area was locked. Did you notice when you were there?"

"I didn't notice. I remember that it was closed, but whether or not it was locked, I don't know. Have you asked Anton?"

"Yes, we have. He didn't remember either. It was not locked when we got there this morning. The other doors were, so presumably the person who stabbed Dr. Mendel left by the back door."

"Unless the other doors had the kind of lock that you can set from the inside and just pull the door shut."

"Both of them had dead bolts as well. Those were locked."

"I notice that you are not saying whether you think the perpetrator was male or female. Does that mean I'm still on your list?"

"Everyone is still on my list."

73

"Okay. He/she may have been either male or female, but whoever did it had been invited into the house by Jon."

"How do you figure that?"

"It's pretty obvious. If someone found the back door unlocked and came in with the intent of killing Jon, he/she would either have brought a weapon or else used something at hand there near the pool. They wouldn't have gone running into the kitchen to get a knife, assuming that they expected to find one easily. And if they did, Jon wouldn't have waited there to be stabbed. There was a door that formerly was a back door to the house, between the pool and the main house. It had a lock on it. I think Jon would have slammed that shut and beat it out onto the lawn. I think he was pretty athletic and could escape from anyone pursuing him. No, he let the person in, headed toward the pool because he had planned to swim, got into a discussion that turned into an argument. That person picked a knife out of the rack and followed Jon."

Tucker smiled. "You'd make a good detective, Dr. McKinnon. That's pretty much the way I figure it."

"Unless the person had a key to the house. Have you located his wife?"

"We have. She was in Vancouver setting up an exhibit of her paintings. She was definitely there. She will be back here on the morning plane."

"Did anyone else have a key?"

"We're looking into that. Now, Doctor, I'm supposed to be the one asking questions."

"Sorry. Fire away."

"How well do you know Niall Raymond?"

"Not well. We're neighbours, but other than that, we move in different circles. He does drop in here for a chat every once in a while. He was here earlier this evening."

"What did he talk about?"

"He doesn't like being considered a suspect."

"Nobody does. Can't be helped. When he came to Dr. Mendel's house last night, what was he wearing?"

"I don't know. I didn't see him. I only heard Jon talking to him. But when he came by tonight, I noticed his shoes. They were those multi-coloured sneakers that are so popular these days."

"Was he home when you got home last night? Any lights on in his house?"

"I didn't see him but I heard him come in later."

"What time?"

"Again, I don't know. I was half asleep when I heard him slam the door. There is no sound insulation in those houses. You can hear everything that goes on next door. I don't know whether I was just falling asleep, in which case it was shortly after midnight, or whether the door slamming woke me up, in which case it could have been any time during the night. Your policeman told you it was some time after eleven thirty. I can't come any closer than that."

"Your husband said he was asleep and didn't see or hear Raymond at all."

"That's right. He was."

"To get back to Dr. Mendel, did you ever get the impression that he used street drugs?"

"No. Absolutely not!"

"How about Raymond?"

"He does. He'd been using them a couple of times when he came in here. Either that or he'd been drinking."

"Do you think he could have been getting his drugs from Mendel?"

"Absolutely not!"

"Or Mendel getting them from Raymond?"

"No!"

"You sound pretty sure of that."

"You can forget about Jon Mendel having anything to do with drugs." I might be sure, but I had the impression Tucker wasn't paying any attention to my denials.

"You think Raymond uses drugs, don't you? You thought your clinic was being used as a drop-off point at one time."

"I know he does. I don't know where he gets them now. Do you?"

"We think there are several places. They may move around from one place to another."

"Well, I don't think it's at this clinic since I fired the kids who used to work here. I think they must have agreed to distribute drugs in order to get their own fix." He nodded his agreement, but went back to his initial line of questioning.

"We are trying to find out what Mendel's connection was to Raymond."

"You should talk to Della Virtue. She'll give you an earful."

"Who is she?"

"The wife of the college treasurer and the college busy body and rumour monger."

"What does she say?"

"She says that Jon was interested in all the other women, and that Jon's wife flirted with all the men. There is no basis for either idea as far as I can tell. I'm just telling you this because I'm sure someone will bring it up, and you shouldn't give it any credence."

"We've already heard things along that line. We'll keep an open mind."

"I hope you do. But to get back to your question, their connection is math. Jon taught real math and Niall thinks everything can be done better with computers. He told me that he wanted to show Jon a new app that just came on the market."

"Is that why he says he went over to Mendel's house last night?"

"Yes."

"Okay, let's put that aside for now. What do you know about Dr. Mendel's relationship with this graduate student, Kent Anderson? Your husband says Anderson was intimidated by Dr. Mendel."

"I don't know anything about their relationship. You'll have to get that information from other faculty members. But I did hear Jon say that he respected Anderson for what he was doing. Other than that, I don't know anything. I've never met Anderson."

Tucker merely nodded.

I thought of Hazel Frick' remark about sending more able police to carry on the investigation.

"By the way, why does Drayford have an independent police force instead of using the RCMP?"

"When the town began to grow, the local council decided they were big boys now and should act like it. Personally, I'm glad. They had the good sense to recruit a really good man from Vancouver to be Chief of Police. I worked with him in Vancouver, and he recruited me. As long as the town can afford to pay him, we will have good policing here. One of these days, he'll move on, and when he does, I'll go with him. I like it here, so I hope the Chief stays. I like the college atmosphere, and I like most of the students I've met. They're mostly farm boys, and quite a few girls, and tend to be honest and practical. I get along with them. There are a few who use drugs, but perhaps less than in other places."

So much for Hazel Frick' complaint about the local force calling in the experts!

President Beliveau ordered the campus flags to be flown at half-mast, and announced that a memorial service for Dr. Jonathon Mendel would be held later in the week, and that all classes would be cancelled at that time so that the students could attend.

Anton told me that his students were subdued when he greeted them on Monday, and expressed their sorrow at the professor's death. One of Anton's brightest students, a big raw-boned cowboy type named Tim McQuarrie, told him that the students, who had all taken Jon's course the previous year, respected him because he made an effort to determine what they really needed and to provide it.

"He scared the hell out of me," McQuarrie said. "He was very demanding, but he gave you credit for doing good work. It made me a better student, and I always went to his classes prepared."

That sounded to me like a pretty good epitaph.

CHAPTER FOURTEEN

Monday morning, when I arrived at our home with the idea of dropping into bed and sleeping all day, the phone was ringing. I recognized the number as that of my granddad. *Oh God, I thought. There goes my day's sleep!* But it was not my granddad on the phone.

"Hello, is this Gail McKinnon?"

"Yes. Who is this?"

"I'm Gordon's neighbour. He asked me to call you and tell you he won't be coming today." I heaved a sigh of relief. The voice went on. "He tripped on a loose rug last night and fell and broke his leg. It's not a bad break, but he has a cast on it and can't get around. He wanted a walking cast, but didn't get it, and he's a bit wobbly with his crutches. I think the doctor didn't give him a walking cast in order to keep him quiet."

"Is he in hospital?"

"No, he's home, but he's sleeping. Don't worry. He has lots of friends here and we'll take care of him."

I'll bet you will if all of you are female! I thought. But I was very glad they were going to keep him occupied at home.

"He says he will call you tomorrow."

And call me he did. The phone was ringing the next morning when I got home. I reassured him that neither Anton nor I had been arrested, and that he had nothing to worry about.

"I'm thankful for that," he said. "I'm having trouble getting used to these crutches. I think I'd better stay home." I heaved a sigh of relief.

The memorial service for Jon Mendel was held on Tuesday afternoon in the gym. There would be a funeral at a date to be set later, once Jon's relatives had been contacted. Anton and I sat near the back so we could survey the crowd. The wannabe girlfriends were both there, both sitting in the front row, but on opposite sides of the room. The looks they gave each other were definitely not friendly. I wondered why they didn't just give up, now that Jon was dead. About ten minutes after the service had started, a young woman clad in a tailored suit in subdued colours eased her way quietly into a seat beside us. It made me think she didn't want to be recognized and I wondered if this was Leah Mendel. She was a small woman with shoulder length dark brown hair expertly waved, brown eyes and a complexion that spoke of much tender loving care. She was beautiful. She wore a ring of sapphire surrounded by diamonds that certainly had not been bought at Wal-Mart. No wonder the single ladies on the campus were so jealous. How this lovely woman who appeared to be in her mid-twenties had captured the heart of an ordinary looking middle-aged man was probably a question that obsessed the single women of the college.

As the service neared its end, she rose and moved toward the door, evidently wanting to get away before the general exodus. I nudged Anton, who had been the one sitting beside her, and whispered, "Let's go talk to her."

We caught up with her outside the door. I asked, "Are you Leah?"

She turned toward us, but hesitated as if she wasn't sure whether to talk to us or not.

"We're Anton and Gail Schild. We were friends of Jon's," I said.

"Oh. You were the people who were visiting him Saturday night, aren't you?" She did not sound antagonistic, so I assumed she did not think we had rewarded his inviting us by sticking a knife into him.

"We only met him recently, but we had come to like him very much. He talked about you with a lot of pride in his voice and showed us your paintings, and we could tell that he loved you very much."

Tears welled up in her eyes and she dabbed at them with a tissue. Anton, who is a real softy, put an arm discreetly around her shoulder and gave a gentle squeeze. "If there is anything we can do for you, please call on us."

"Thank you. I would like to talk to you someday, but right now, I feel I want to be alone."

"At least let us walk with you. Are you going to your house?"

"No. I can't face it yet. I parked in the lot just inside the gate. I am staying at a hotel for the time being."

"Are you sure you want to be alone? Do you have other friends here?"

"Not really. Lots of acquaintances, but no one really close. I'm sorry. I don't mean to be stuck up. I do really want to get to know you. You see, Jon called me Saturday night and told me about you."

"Saturday night?" I asked.

"Yes. After you'd left. It wasn't that late. I was in Vancouver, so our time was an hour earlier than here and he knew I work late, so ten wasn't really late. He said he'd met some really interesting people he wanted me to get to know when I got through in Vancouver and got home. I was setting up for an exhibit of my art, which will be the end of this month."

"You were there all month for that?"

"Yes. I'll admit that we had a quarrel and I left earlier than I needed to. It wasn't about either of us thinking the other was too friendly with people of the opposite sex. That's not true. It was because I felt sort of stifled here. I didn't fit in. And I missed the cultural activity of Vancouver. I wanted him to leave and go back home. But I came to realize how much he enjoyed what he was doing. It gave him a feeling of doing something really useful. We both were sorry we'd quarreled, and we'd made up. He told me he would see about things like concerts that we could go to in Calgary. It has a symphony orchestra that plays in a hall with a really good organ. We also talked about finding out whether there was anything exciting going on at Banff Centre at spring break time. He came down to visit me a couple of times and we talked about it. I'm glad we made up. I would hate it if we hadn't made up before he died. I really do love him."

"He felt the same about you."

We walked a ways farther before she spoke again. "I know when his killer came to the house."

"How's that?"

"We talked about fifteen or twenty minutes. He told me all about you two. Then I could hear the doorbell ring and he said, 'I'll call you tomorrow,' and hung up. It must have been the person who killed him who came to the door."

"Where were we fifteen or twenty minutes after we left Jon?" I asked after we had parted from Leah Mendel.

"Probably longer that that. He wouldn't have gone right to the phone," Anton reminded me. "Say eleven fifteen. Were we still talking to the man with the dog?"

"Probably not. I'd say we were watching the lights on the fountain."

"Anyway, we couldn't have made it back to Jon's house in time. I think that's our line of defense, in case Tucker still suspects us."

While we had our heads together discussing timetables, we almost literally ran into Della Virtue. "Oh there you are Mrs. Shields," she shouted. "I still haven't heard from you about what you're going to bring to the potluck tonight. Do you know where Anna Hopkins lives? I can draw you a map."

For comic relief, this took the cake.

"I told you I wasn't coming. I will be working at my veterinary clinic. And I'm not interested anyway."

"You're making a mistake if you keep taking that attitude. You will find that it will be hard for you to fit in on this campus if you don't get involved in campus activities."

"I don't think I have any requirement to fit in. I have my own profession."

"Well don't tell me I didn't warn you." She stalked off in a huff.

I turned toward Anton and found him doubled over, laughing.

"What's so funny?" someone behind us asked.

We turned around to find Sgt. Tucker striding toward us. "I saw you talking to Leah Mendel. Was she at the memorial service? I didn't think I should go."

"Yes, she came in very quietly and sat in the back. I don't think she wants to meet the locals just now." I told him. "And I don't blame her, with all the gossip going around."

"She will have to put up with it eventually."

"I suppose she'll go back to Vancouver. I don't think she has any personal connection with Drayford."

"You're right. She told me she would move back to Vancouver and put the house up for sale."

"Did she tell you about the phone call she had with Jon on Saturday night, after we'd left?"

"She did. It gives us a time frame for the murder. And it agrees with the pathologists report on the state of rigor mortis."

"But that doesn't necessarily mean that the person who rang the doorbell was the one who killed him," Anton remarked. "Rigor might depend on environmental factors. He was immersed in water from the time he was killed until we found him."

"I am aware of that. But we took the temperature of the water in the pool. It was about the same as normal household temperature. It probably didn't affect the rigor."

Anton conceded the argument, then went on, "We were trying to figure out where we were at the time that call ended and someone came to the door. We think we were standing by the fountain watching the lights make the water droplets sparkle."

Tucker only nodded.

CHAPTER FIFTEEN

"I'd better change my pants," Anton said when we got home. "These are looking a bit grubby." On Sunday afternoon the police had come to collect the clothing we were wearing the night before when we visited Jon. Anton had hastily emptied the pockets of the pants he had been wearing that night and stuffed things into the ones of the pair he was wearing on Sunday. Now he emptied the contents of his pockets, and besides the usual collection of odds and ends that accumulate in a guy's pockets, a small piece of paper fell out and drifted down to the floor. He picked it up, glanced at it, then studied it more carefully, a perplexed expression on his face.

"What's the matter?" I asked.

"I don't know where this note came from." He handed it to me.

"Maybe you picked it up at Jon's. 'Call P. Ormond.' Is there a P. Ormond here at the college?"

"I don't know. I must have picked it up with the change that fell out of my pocket when I was dressing. I remember that there was a note on his bedside table." He got the college directory and looked through it. "Not here."

In the meantime, I looked through the telephone directory. "It isn't anyone who lives in the Drayford area."

"Now I'm curious. You know, this might be important. He probably hadn't made that call yet, since he left the message sitting there."

"Yes, it might. And you know what this means, don't you?"

"What?"

"It means that you have absconded with a piece of evidence that might be important. I wish you had noticed it before now. That might make the police think we had deliberately taken something important from the scene of a crime."

"God. I never thought of that. And we said we were going to keep our noses clean." We stared at each other in consternation.

"Look," I said. "If I'm no busier tonight than I have been so far, I can pull up phone directories on the tablet at work and look for the name. It's not a common one like Smith or Johnson. If we can locate the person, we could call and see who it is, and maybe find out what Jon was calling about."

"We really should give it to Sgt. Tucker."

"Yeah, we should have done that on Sunday. We can't very well give it to them now. They'll think we were holding it back on purpose. I think they still suspect us, even if they are treating us kindly."

"Yeah, you're right. I'll come with you and bring my tablet. We can check all the directories in Alberta if we need to."

As we perused the directories of every town in Alberta that evening, we speculated on who P. Ormond might be.

"The police think Jon might have been connected in some way with the drug scene here in town," Anton commented.

I snorted. "He's not a user, that's for sure. I didn't see any signs that he used drugs either at the President's reception, or on Saturday night, and I'm sure they have done tests. If they'd been positive, the police would be concentrating on that, and they're not. It's just an idea they have about why he might have been killed. And if you want to see a druggy, you should see Niall at one o'clock in the morning. He stops by to visit, and a couple of times, he's been stoned. I wonder what his connection is with Jon."

"He comes over to see Jon's wife."

"Not likely. He's not dumb. He comes over to the Mendel house on days when Leah isn't there. Niall is smart enough to have found out when the lady is gone and not bother visiting. "

"Maybe he's just pretending to be dumb. The police must think he is. They think he does have something going with Leah. I wonder if he just says that as a diversion so we wouldn't think of something else. Hey, I haven't found any P. Ormond in any of the towns I've checked."

"I haven't either. Let's try BC. Jon came from the Vancouver area. Why don't you take the 250 numbers, and I'll take the 604 ones."

"Okay."

After about twenty minutes of searching, Anton exclaimed, "I've found him!"

"Oh, good. Who is it?"

I peered over his shoulder as he read out the name. "Ormond, Percy, Right Reverend."

"A *bishop*?"

"Yes, a bishop." We stared at each other. "Well, that does away with our idea of Jon's drug dealer, doesn't it?"

"I should hope so. I wonder what kind of church."

"Let's look in the yellow pages under churches. Where there's a bishop, there's a cathedral."

Our search was quick. The first entry under Anglican was that of The Cathedral Church of St. Peter and St. Paul. There were no other cathedrals listed.

"He won't have his office at the cathedral. Let's see if we can find another listing," I suggested. A few lines down, we found Diocese of Chilcotin, Synod Office. "That will be it." The number was not the one after Bishop Ormond's name. That must be his home number, we reasoned.

"Do you think we should call him at home, or wait till tomorrow and call the Synod office?" Anton asked.

"He might not be in his office tomorrow. I think we try him tonight. If we get him, what do we ask?"

"I think we tell the truth," Anton reasoned.

"You call him. He might talk to a man more readily than a woman."

He grinned at me. "That's sexist."

"So what?" I retorted.

He picked up the phone and was about to dial on the private line, rather than the clinic's listed one. He hesitated. "What do you call a bishop?"

"'My Lord.' But I doubt if many Canadian bishops use that title."

It was no surprise to us that what we got was voice mail. "Should I leave a message?" Anton wondered.

"I think so."

So Anton, putting on his most authoritative tone of voice, said into the phone, "This is Dr. Anton Schild, calling from Drayford, Alberta. We will call again tomorrow morning." He did not leave our number, but less than thirty minutes later the private line rang. Picking up the phone, I put it on speaker-phone and answered, "This is Dr. Gail Schild."

A rich basso voice answered, "I found a message from Dr. Anton Schild on my voice mail. This is Percy Ormond."

"Anton is my husband. He's here on the line also."

"What can I do for you?"

Anton took over. "We are calling from Drayford College in Drayford Alberta. Are you acquainted with Professor Jon Mendel?"

"Oh yes. He used to be one of my parishioners before I was elected bishop."

"Are you aware that he is dead? In fact, he has been murdered."

There was a long silence on the line. When the bishop answered, his voice was low and sounded distressed. "No. I didn't know. When did this happen?"

"Apparently late Saturday night. Gail and I had dinner with him that night. We left about ten thirty. He then evidently decided to go for a swim in his private pool and someone stabbed him. His body was found Sunday morning in the pool. In fact I was partly responsible for finding it."

"How dreadful for you."

"Yes. But as a result of being the last people to see Jon alive, we automatically became suspects. We aren't worried about that, but today I discovered that I had inadvertently picked up a message and took it away with me. It said 'call P. Ormond' and we wonder whether it was a critical piece of evidence. But if we take it to the police now, they will think we are trying to hide something and we will be even more suspect. So we thought we'd call you to see what Jon's call might be about."

"I can't imagine that anything he would have called me about would be evidence in his murder."

"If we could be sure of that, we wouldn't hesitate to give them the note. We thought he might be returning your call, or that it might be something quite mundane."

"I see you do have a problem. But I don't think I can help you. I have no idea what he was calling about. I'll tell you what I will do. I would like to know what happened to him as much as you do. He was a very good friend. I'll come to Drayford. I will check with the police and tell them only that I received word of his death. Once they talk to me, there will probably be no importance to that message anyway. But don't destroy it."

"No. We won't do that."

"I can't come tomorrow. I will make plans to come Thursday. I will call you back to let you know."

I got into the conversation. "This is a number at my veterinary clinic. If you call tomorrow, call our home phone." I gave him the number.

He did not wait until the next day. Half an hour later, he called back.

"I'll come on the commuter flight that gets into Drayford at five pm. Can you meet me?"

"Certainly," I replied.

"Can we talk somewhere before I show up in the town to talk to police?"

"We can come here to the clinic. It's an emergency clinic and doesn't open until seven."

"Good. Are you both veterinarians?"

"No. Anton is on the faculty of the college."

"Well, if you were friends of Jon, I will look forward to meeting you."

The commuter flight touched down at Drayford's newly improved airport right on time. There were several people waiting to board it for the return flight to Calgary. I was sizing them up and deciding that these were people from the college or paleontologists from the museum, not farmers, when Anton remarked, "Well, that answers that question."

"What question?"

"How a boy named Percy could survive being bullied in school."

I looked toward the people walking toward the terminal from the plane. Among them, wearing the purple shirt, clerical collar and pectoral cross of a bishop was a man about six and a half feet tall, with bull neck, broad shoulders, barrel chest and a head of closely cropped salt and pepper hair. He looked like a defensive lineman on a professional football team. He shook hands with us, gathered his bag and followed us to the car. The old Vibe sank down on the passenger side as he lowered himself onto the seat.

We drove to the clinic, locked the door after us and went into my office, taking a spare chair from the waiting room. The bishop wasted no time getting down to business.

"I have obtained accounts of Jon's murder on the internet. Do you think the newspaper accounts are accurate?"

"Reasonably so," I responded. "The police are not releasing much information, but what they did give reporters seems to be reported fairly accurately."

"All right. Now tell me about your connection with what happened."

Anton was the one who took up the narrative. "First, let me tell you about the fountain. It has an automatic timer that shuts it off and drains the pool early on Sunday mornings, so the maintenance people can clean the pool. I go for an early morning run every day, and as I passed the fountain on Sunday, I saw police cars there. I stopped to see what was going on. The police and the maintenance men were looking at a knife that had apparently been thrown into the pool. It had what looked like clotted blood on it where the blade joins the handle. I recognized the knife as one of a set Jon had shown us when we were at his house for dinner. He said it was a very superior set, made of German steel, and that it kept its sharp edge much better than most knives. He had his initials engrave on the handle."

"Is this a knife he was using while you were there?"

"No," I said. "It was a filet knife. He didn't use it that night. I was watching him chop up things for dinner, but he was using another one from the set. I was admiring the blade, which seem to cut effortlessly, and the beautiful handle."

"Was anyone else there that night?"

"No we were the only guests, but another man came by. He is actually our neighbor at the college housing. He said that since Jon had company, he would come back later. We don't know whether he meant later that night or another day, but he told the police it was just a commonplace comment that didn't mean any specific time."

"That seems reasonable. You said you went with the police to Jon's house."

Anton replied, "Yes. I told them we'd been visiting Jon the previous night, so we became immediate suspects, and I don't think the cops wanted to let me out of their sight. They told me to call Gail and have her come over, too."

"It must have been very distressful to you."

"It certainly was! But they let me help fish his body out of the pool, and having something to do helped me keep going."

"Now, let me see this note you found. By the way, why were you sure it had been written by Jon?"

I replied, "While I was in the kitchen with him, I saw him make a note of something to get the next time he went to the grocery store, on a pad he kept there. I noticed his writing. It was distinctive. So when I looked at the note Anton had picked up, I recognized the writing."

Bishop Ormond nodded. "I can't think of anything he would be calling me about. It may have been just a social call."

"But why would he have made a note to call you?"

"That's the question, isn't it?"

"What would he be likely to call his parish priest for advice about?"

"I can't remember him ever asking my advice on personal questions. We had many talks about theology, ethics and other subjects, but he was very introspective when it came to his personal affairs."

"There was rumour about his wife showing interest in another man, and I know of at least two women here who have an interest in him."

"I didn't know his wife. He was married after I left the parish. But I don't think he would turn to anyone else for advice on anything like that. He would have dealt with it himself."

"Is there anything that might cause him to do so, some major problem that was new?"

"That's always a possibility of course."

I had been considering another possibility and decided I'd better speak my mind. I asked the bishop, "What was Jon's attitude toward homosexuals?"

"He was opposed to discrimination toward them. He had the modern attitude that they were children of God, who happened to be different. Why do you ask?"

"The man who came over on Saturday night while we were there asked if Leah, Jon's wife, was there. He should have known that Leah was away. I wonder if he had actually come to see Jon and didn't want to admit it in front of Jon's company."

"You think this man might have been gay and was propositioning Jon?"

"Yes. And had been doing so for a while."

"I think Jon would have bluntly told him to get lost."

"But what if Jon had found himself developing an interest. Would that upset him enough that he might call his trusted priest for advice?"

"Gail, what made you think that?" Anton asked.

"Anton dear, didn't you notice that while we were swimming Saturday night, he never took his eyes off you? You do have a beautiful body."

Anton turned scarlet with embarrassment and the bishop's eyes crinkled at the corners as he smiled in amusement.

"Gail, you are the one men are attracted by."

"Usually. I admit that I have noticed that. But Jon didn't. He had his eyes on you, not me."

Bishop Ormond became serious again. "*If* that was so, yes he might find himself out of his depth and want advice. But I wonder if you are perhaps imagining his interest in your husband." With that remark, he rose. "I think it's time I turned up at the police station to let them know I'm here. I won't mention the note. I don't think it will be necessary."

After he left, I said to Anton, "I wonder if he really thinks the note is not important or whether he doesn't want the possibility of Jon being gay to become public knowledge."

"I don't know. But I think we'd better hang onto that note."

CHAPTER SIXTEEN

The weather remained warm and sunny through that week, though a change was forecast for the weekend. I had three days off starting on Friday, so I took a short nap when I got home from the clinic that morning, then fixed a lunch for us to eat in the grassy inner circle of the campus. Anton met me there and we found a bench in the warm sunlight. Tim MacQuarrie, the cowboy type who had praised Jon Mendel to Anton, came by and stopped to talk to Anton, who introduced me.

"I'm pleased to meet you Dr. McKinnon. A buddy of mine took his dog in to see you the other night, and he was very happy with the way you treated him." He turned to Anton and went on, "I was on my way to the Corral but I wanted to talk to you some time. I hope I'm not interrupting you." The Corral was the student union building.

"Not at all," Anton replied.

Tim squatted on his heels, cowboy fashion, facing us. "It's about what they're saying about Leah Mendel. I know you were friends of Dr. Mendel. Did you ever meet Leah?"

"We hadn't until Tuesday. She was at the memorial service. We only got here a few days before classes started."

"I imagine Dr. Mendel told you he had open house for students every night of the week. You could drop in and talk to him about your classes or something that worried you or whatever was on your mind. Leah was always really friendly and had some goodies for us to munch on, or left us in private to talk to Dr. Mendel, whatever you wanted. All this talk about her flirting with all the men on campus is a bunch of bunk. She was just a friendly person, and I think she felt that she should help her husband by making the students welcome. Do you get what I'm saying?"

"Yes I do."

"Well, anyway, I think she also liked being around younger people. She told me once that she'd gone to a meeting of the faculty wives and decided it wasn't for her and never went again."

I laughed. "I know what she meant. I've had the same experience."

Tim smiled at me. "Then you know what I'm talking about. I think some of those ladies are just trying to give Leah a bad time."

"But you call Mrs. Mendel by her first name. Don't you think that has something to do with their reaction?" I suggested.

"She told us to. We call Dr. Mendel by his title, because that's how he introduced himself at the beginning of the class. He was a bit formal, actually. Some of the profs expect to be called either Doctor or Professor, but others go by first names and are more chummy with the students. I just respond to them the way they introduce themselves."

"That sounds like a good plan."

Tim turned back toward Anton. "I'm wondering about the kids who are taking Dr. Mendel's course. Dr. Hopkins is teaching it now. He's the department head, but he's a pure mathematician. He thinks calculus and trig are the most beautiful things in the world. He's not a farmer, but for that matter neither was Dr. Mendel. Anyway, I wonder whether he can put it across. And to get back to the Mendels' open house, I once told Dr. Mendel that I was trying to devise a course for high school students based on his course. Not all farm kids go on to college, but they still need to know how to do the bookkeeping for the farm. He encouraged me and asked me to work on it over the summer and show it to him this fall. I did so, and I showed it to him at the open house one night, and he gave me some tips and said to keep working on it."

"That's great, Tim," Anton remarked. "I wonder if you might be able to help Hopkins with the course. Why don't you ask him and show him your plan and see what he says."

"D'you think he would pay any attention to me? I mean, I'm only a third year student."

"My impression of Charlie Hopkins is that he is a man who would take you seriously. He might be glad of your help. Why don't you ask? He won't bite you."

"Okay, I guess I should. Thanks a lot Dr. Schild."

After Tim had gone on his way, I said to Anton, "Now I know you're going to be a formal old fuddy-duddy. He called you Dr. Schild. Is being a professor going to go to your head?"

"It might, if I ever get to being a professor," he retorted. "He also called you Dr. McKinnon, so you'll never be like your pal, Tom Grant, whose clients all call him by his first name."

He was right about that. I'm proud of my doctor's degree and resent people who will call a male vet "Doctor" but call a female one "Missus." I'm also annoyed when I go to trade shows and salesman ask to talk to my husband, assuming I'm the vet's wife. Maybe I should send my husband, Dr. Schild, over to talk to them about the genetics of cereal grains.

Later that afternoon, the phone rang. "This is Percy Ormond. I am about to leave, but wanted to let you know that I don't think you have anything to worry about in regard to that note. I have talked extensively with Sgt. Tucker, who was not at all curious about how I happened to be here. He thought it quite normal, which in fact it is. I want to thank you for calling me. I don't know anyone else here who would have thought of informing me, so I might not have known of his death for some time."

"Do you need a ride out to the airport?" I asked.

"No, the local priest will take me. I will come back for the funeral. A date has not been set yet, but the local priest has asked me if I'd like to officiate. I think he is a bit reluctant to do a funeral for a murder victim, especially one he didn't know. I am happy to do so. We called the bishop of this diocese to obtain his permission and he graciously granted it."

"Why did you need his permission?"

"I am not a priest of this diocese. Anyone who comes from outside the diocese must get the local bishop's permission. It is frequently done, and I know the Bishop of Calgary quite well. There are not many of us in the bishop business, so we all know one another."

"Didn't Jon go to the local church? I know there is an Anglican church. I am culturally an Anglican and Anton is Lutheran, so we thought we'd go one week to the local Lutheran church and another week to the Anglican. We went to the Lutheran Church a couple of weeks ago and liked it. The pastor is young and is in tune with the students. It is a very vibrant congregation. We were planning on going to the Anglican Church last Sunday, but of course we didn't."

"Yes, Jon told me recently in an e-mail that he had gone once since the new rector arrived, but had not gone back. The new man was chosen by the older members of the parish, who still control the church. They didn't allow younger, newer members on the selection committee. They chose a priest who was as much like the old rector as possible, very old school, preferring the Book of Common Prayer to the Book of Alternative Services, and hymns from the old hymnbook. There's nothing wrong with that, but Jon didn't feel at home there."

"I can imagine that if he had liked the new rector, he'd have had the man over to dinner and gotten acquainted. He would probably have enjoyed a good discussion on theology."

"Yes, he would."

CHAPTER SEVENTEEN

I had Friday, Saturday and Sunday nights off, and we planned our first entire weekend in which we could do things together by taking part in college and town activities. On Saturday afternoon, the red and gold Dragons would play a rugby game against a town team dressed, appropriately, in black and blue. Drayford was not a large enough school to have a Canadian football team, but a rugby team is much less expensive to outfit. On Sunday night, we would attend a Community Concert programme, featuring a well-known pianist, to be held at the Town Hall. We had bought series tickets for the year. If I couldn't go to one of the concerts, Anton would give my ticket to a student.

The weather forecast for the weekend showed a front moving in. It would bring cloud cover on Saturday, with rain starting by Sunday. Friday would be the last clear day for a while. The moon was two days away from the full moon, so on Friday Anton suggested that we should drive down the river and see the hoodoos in the moonlight.

We had to drive through town to reach the turnoff for the highway that led down the river. This took us past the clinic, and as we passed it I noticed that the exterior light that illuminated the sign was not on. Nor was the light in the waiting room. I asked Anton to stop. I got out and went to the door, finding it locked. I pulled out my key, opened the door, turned on the lights and walked purposefully into the treatment room, where to my surprise, I found Kevin and Shawna just leaving my office which opened into the treatment room.

"What are you doing here?" I demanded.

"Irwin hired us. He's on duty tonight," Kevin replied sullenly.

"Where is he?" I had not seen any sign of Dr. Prouse.

"Oh, he only comes down if there's a call he has to take. He hasn't had any tonight," Shawna replied.

I walked into the office and found the safe wide open. I whirled toward the two kids. "Who opened the safe?"

There was a hesitation before Shawna muttered, "Oh, Irwin left it open."

"You said he hadn't been here this evening."

Again the hesitation. "Oh, he was here earlier."

I knew she was lying. "You said he hadn't been here. Was he or wasn't he?"

Kevin interrupted belligerently, "Nothing's missing from the safe. You can see for yourself."

I went to the safe and checked the contents. I keep a daily record of the drugs stored there, so that I can tell if one of the other vets has used some, in case I need to order more. I checked my log and counted vials of morphine. All that were supposed to be there were. The euthanasia solution had the correct amount remaining in the bottle. A box of vials of a different narcotic that I prefer for cats was still unopened, its seal intact. So was a supply of Naloxone. We don't use much of that narcotic antagonist, but an occasional animal reacts excessively to what would normally be a proper dose of morphine. As well, in dogs and cats, an overdose can bring on convulsions. There is also the possibility that one of the druggies on the street might give some of their stuff to their dog. I've seen dogs that have been given stranger things than that by their owners. At Guelph, I had the opportunity to take a course given to paramedics, firefighters and police on the use of Naloxone. The local vet society sponsored a seminar on our legal rights and responsibilities in using the stuff.

The log showed that no one else had used any of the controlled substances. Irwin Prouse, who might or might not have been there earlier in the evening, had not made an entry in the log. Everything looked normal. I swung the door shut and spun the combination to lock it. I felt certain that these kids knew the combination and had opened the safe themselves; for what reason, I had no idea. I resolved to talk to Alex Breling the next time I could get hold of him and ask to have the combination changed. I hoped that it would be possible to do so. It was an old safe. I wondered whether the company that made it would even be in existence any more.

I'd worry about that later, I decided. Tonight, Anton and I were just going on an exploration of our new home base.

The moonlight was brilliant in the clear prairie air. We could see the hoodoos from quite a ways off. Anton pulled into the parking lot, but seeing that the road went a bit farther, he continued on. Almost immediately he saw that it only led to a turnaround, so he backed up into a parking space, facing out. He got out and started to walk toward the base of the hillside. The hoodoos, towers of compact soil, each topped by a large flat rock, cast weird shadows along the side of the valley. These odd formations are caused by erosion over thousands or even millions of years washing away the soil except where a rock has kept it from doing so. Eventually these towers of soil will collapse, but we probably won't still be around to see it.

I got out of the passenger side of the car, and as I did so, I saw a bright reflection from something shiny behind some low shrubs. Curious, I went over to investigate. It was a shiny blue mountain bike with saddlebags slung across the rear wheel. I recognized it immediately as the one that I had seen Billy, the man I thought might be a drug dealer, riding. What was he doing out here? I hurried to catch up with Anton, not wanting to shout to him about my find. I felt uneasy. I didn't trust Billy, and this was a pretty isolated place at this time of night.

I had only gone a few steps when I saw Anton, who had started up the hillside toward the first hoodoos, stop and look up toward the top of the slope that held the strange formations. I followed his glance and saw a shadowy figure scurry from behind one hoodoo and disappear behind another.

"Hello!" Anton called out in a loud, carrying voice. He stood still, waiting for an answer, I assumed. Silence reigned.

Anton started to move up the trail again, going slowly. There was no more movement of anyone farther up the slope. Anton called out again. Again no answer. He moved farther up the trail. Suddenly, I saw a flash and heard the sharp crack of a gunshot. Anton hesitated for only a second, then spun and started to run. He is as courageous as anyone, but when you are standing in bright moonlight, with nowhere to hide, and someone is taking potshots at you from a place of concealment, with the advantage of higher ground, the only reasonable thing to do is to get out of there. Two more shots rang out.

I ran back to the car, jumped into the driver's side and roared out of the parking spot, back toward the turnaround at the end of the road. I hadn't latched the passenger door, and as I flung the car into a skidding turn, the door flew open. Anton lunged into the passenger seat and pulled his legs in after him. He pulled the door shut as I spun the tires getting out of there. I didn't stop until we were out on the highway, beyond reach of anyone on foot with a gun.

We stared at each other, then simultaneously asked, "You okay?"

I added, "Did any of those shots hit you?"

"No. The first one pinged off a rock about two feet away. And I saw one send up a spurt of dirt near me when I was running. He was either a bad shot, or he wasn't trying to hit me, just scare me. He did that all right. Even if he wasn't trying to hit me, any one of those shots could have ricocheted off a rock."

"What do you think he was trying to do up there? Could you tell? You were closer to him than I was. I only saw a dim figure dashing from one place to another."

"He had something in his hand when I first saw him, but he crouched down and left it behind the top hoodoo before he ran to the other one. He didn't have anything in his hand when he ran over there. I thought he might be a vandal, wanting to damage the hoodoos."

"He wasn't," I told Anton. "While you were walking over there, I saw Billy's bicycle hidden in the bushes. I was trying to catch up with you to warn you. I think this might be one of his drop-off points. And I think we'd better get going. He could catch us on his bike."

"Billy? The guy you think is a drug dealer?"

"Yeah."

"Let's go!"

As we drove back to town, we discussed whether we should report the incident. Would we be believed? We had no proof. And one of my clients, chatting while I worked on his dog, told me that Billy was the son of one of the town council members. He saw Billy poke his head in to talk to Kevin and had remarked that Billy had been a disappointment to his father, a local lawyer. The father wanted his son to study law, but the son had gone to the University of Calgary for one year, then quit. He worked in the lumberyard of Drayford Hardware and seemed to have no interest in further education. My client wondered where Billy had gotten the money to buy the fancy bike. I had my own idea about where the money came from, but thought it better not to say so to the client. Maybe his father gave him the bike, I suggested.

I related this conversation to Anton and he was even more reluctant to report the incident, even though he was the one who had been shot at.

The question was settled for us as we entered town. We had only gone a few blocks when a siren sounding behind us made me pull over to let a fire truck pass. Another followed it. I moved forward another block and had to pull over again to let a police car by. We could see the main intersection of the highway and Main Street ahead. A car was overturned. A pickup truck seemed to be trying to climb a power pole. Another car was slewed across one lane. Fire engines, police cars and ambulances were streaming toward the site of the crash. People were running toward the wrecked vehicles. We could hear screaming.

Anton remarked, "We might as well forget going to the police. Every one of them who's on duty will be helping with the crash." I agreed. I turned down the next street and drove along it for several blocks before turning back onto Main Street. We went home and put off the visit to the police until the next morning.

CHAPTER EIGHTEEN

We slept late the next morning. Even Anton failed to get off on his morning run until six o'clock. He wasn't back yet when I left to drive down to the clinic to see what shape it was in. It was a few minutes before seven when I parked in front of the clinic. The lights were all off, the door locked, and no one was around. I had figured it would be that way, so was not surprised.

The schedule book and receipt book showed no entries, which was unusual, as it had begun to get busy in the evenings. I went to my office to check the safe. It was closed and locked. I opened it and again inventoried the contents. Nothing was missing. But someone had been into the safe. All my normal drugs were shoved into the back and there was nothing up front. I always left the drugs near the front so I could get at them easily, and I had done that when I inventoried the contents the night before. Something else must have been placed in the safe, and removed before morning. Was this the place where Kevin and Shawna stashed drugs provided to them by Billy? Were they the minor dealers who then handed the drugs out to select customers? If so, Niall Raymond was one of them. Had Jon Mendel been another? I knew that the police were still thinking along those lines, even though I felt certain that Jon had not been involved in any way with drugs.

Confirmation that the clinic was used as a drop-off for drugs was evident moments later when I found Shawna's cell phone lying on my desk. This was not the first time she had forgotten to take her phone when she left. I recognized it by its purple colour. I punched a button and a text message came up on the screen.

that vet & hr hsbnd no 2 much I cant use the clnc any mor pick up at musim sat 9.30 from usual plas

So I'd been right! My clinic was being used as a place where Billy dropped off the drugs, which were then doled out to other customers. And the message indicated that there were other drop-off points. The hoodoos were probably used for that purpose, and Billy was out there to leave a cache of drugs behind one of the formations. Now we had some definite proof. Should I take Shawna's phone to the police?

I heard the front door open and quickly turned off the phone, leaving it lying on the desk. Shawna popped her head around the corner.

"Is my phone here? Oh, there it is!"

She grabbed the phone and as she turned to leave, she noticed that the safe was open.

"We didn't take anything," she said defensively.

"I see that." Should I question her about what might have been placed in it? No. Leave that to the police, I decided. Shawna scurried out.

While we ate breakfast, I told Anton about what I had found out.

"Unfortunately I didn't have a chance to copy the message on Shawna's phone."

"Which means," Anton replied, "we still don't have any concrete proof. Look, I've been thinking. I'd really like to get to the bottom of this drug business. I can't believe that Jon had anything to do with it, but the police are still questioning people about it. I've heard from a couple of Jon's students, who have gone to Jon's open house, that they've been asked whether they saw any indication of drugs. The police seem to think that the fact that Jon had his house open for students to drop in was a cover-up for dealing drugs."

"I don't believe that!"

"Neither do I. Why don't we go out to the museum tonight and see if we can find those kids picking up drugs there. Or do you think that nine thirty means morning instead of evening?"

"I don't think so. There would be too many people around. The museum must open at about that time. Also, Billy seems to do his drop-offs in the evenings. And he works days at the hardware store. I don't know whether he works weekends, but he could."

"Yeah. I think you're right.

"I'm all for going out there, but it will be dangerous."

"I know."

"You're the one who got shot at last night. But if you're game, I'll go along."

"Okay. We'll go."

The day seemed long and we were impatient to start our stealthy sleuthing expedition, but it wasn't something we could hurry up. We went to the rugby match and enjoyed it, even though the inexperienced Dragons got thumped by the town team, especially by a middle-aged, bald-headed man who was deadly at kicking the ball between the goalposts.

After the game, the members of the two teams shook hands, put on their jackets, and trotted together across the highway to the pub conveniently located there. They were still wearing their uniforms, which consisted of shorts, T-shirt and cleated boots, now covered with dirt and grass stains. They relived the game, the town team joshing the college boys for some of their inexpert play, all done in the best of good humour. Many of the fans, ourselves included, went along with them.

Having gorged on hotdogs during the game, we didn't have much appetite for supper, and at about nine o'clock, we dressed in dark clothes, and set out to play James Bond.

CHAPTER NINETEEN

Clouds had rolled in during the afternoon, and by nine thirty it was quite dark. We parked in a layby below the museum rather than driving up to the parking lot. There was a service road around the back of the museum, so we walked up this road to the area behind the museum where supplies, as well as transported dinosaur skeletons were unloaded. Kevin's old rattletrap was parked there. On our earlier trip to the museum, we had been shown the working area where the exhibits were put together. Granddad's influence had gotten us this tour of the non-public areas. We knew that there was a large shop at the corner of the building, and we could see a light coming from it. On rounding the corner, we found the door wide open and boldly walked in.

A man we recognized as a technician named Jake who helped assemble the exhibits was working in the shop. He did not appear to recognize us, but didn't seem surprised to see strangers arriving at night in his doorway. He glanced up, then returned to his work. A large sliding door opened into a wide hallway, and on the opposite wall another large door provided entrance to the floor where the dioramas were displayed. Perhaps Jake thought we were Kevin and Shawna.

But that idea was squelched when we heard Kevin's voice from the exhibit floor.

There was no light in the hallway but the exhibit floor was dimly illuminated by security lights high up on the walls. We stepped into the huge room, stopping to let our eyes adjust to the dimness. Kevin and Shawna were somewhere among the displays, but we did not spot them until Kevin spoke again.

"I remember it being down this way."

"Are you sure?" Shawna asked.

"Yeah, I think so."

"I'll wait at the door." She turned toward the door and saw us. She let out a yell, and Kevin spun around.

"I'll take her," I said to Anton. "You go get him."

Shawna turned to run, away from the area where Kevin was trying to move back into the shadows. I'm a pretty good athlete, and Shawna probably rarely gets off the couch. I gained ground rapidly. She headed up the sloping ramp toward the ocean exhibits. Suddenly the entire room was flooded with light. The sunken ocean under the Plexiglass floor was just ahead. Shawna put on the brakes, sliding to an awkward stop. This was my chance. Remembering the way the rugby players tackled their opponents, I dived for her legs, wrapping my arms around her thighs and locking them by grabbing one wrist with the other hand. Shawna came crashing down. I pulled my knees under me and hoisted myself toward her, grabbing her right arm and twisting it behind her back. She let out a squeal of pain.

"Get up and I'll let up on your arm. Don't try anything or I'll twist your arm tighter."

Shawna climbed to her feet and I frog-marched her toward the door into the hallway. As we came down the ramp, I could hear a commotion in the far end of the exhibit floor. A man called out, "What's going on here?" Looking toward the sound, I recognized the large, imposing form of a man I only knew as Leo, who worked for SOS Security, standing at the main doorway into the exhibit, his hand still on the light switches.

"These kids came here to pick up some drugs left here for them," I called out.

"Is that Dr. McKinnon?"

"Yeah," I answered. "Anton is down there trying to catch the other one."

Anton was facing a huge T. Rex, and on the other side stood Kevin. Every time Kevin tried to move to get away, Anton moved to cut him off. Kevin would return to his spot behind the dino, alert for another opportunity to get away. A cat and mouse confrontation continued for another minute, then Leo moved in. With someone approaching him from each side, Kevin made a break for it. Anton is very agile and it was only a few moments before he caught the fleeing youth, grasping both arms from behind him and pushing him toward the door to the hallway. We escorted our captives to the shop, Leo following behind and shutting the door to the shop after us.

"Now, let's hear what this is all about," Leo demanded in a firm voice.

Anton explained, "We knew that a drug dealer was using Gail's clinic as a drop-off point, and that these two kids were small-time distributors. Then Gail learned that the guy who supplies them was afraid to use the clinic any more and told these two to go back to using this place as the drop-off point. It had been used that way before the vets started the clinic. So we thought we'd come out here and see if we could catch them in the act. I saw this guy drop a package and kick it under one of the dinos when I first went after him. I can show you where it is."

"Wait till the Mounties come. I called them," Leo replied.

"How did you happen to turn up here?" I asked Leo.

"I saw an old car drive up the back road, then yours stop by the side of the road and saw you walk up here. I wondered what was going on."

We stood around waiting for several more minutes before we heard sirens, and soon two men from the RCMP came in the door. This being outside the city limits, the policing was done by the Mounties. We had to explain the whole thing to them again, and Anton and I had to verify who we were. The fact that Leo knew me and had met Anton one time when he was visiting me at the clinic helped to get us on good terms with the cops. The two kids denied everything, until one of the Mounties asked Leo to escort Anton to the place where he said Kevin had hidden the package. Leo came back holding a small manila envelope. On being opened, this turned out to contain several small zip-lock bags containing a fine powder. The kids lost their aggressiveness and refused to talk. But when I repeated our statement that we had learned that a drop-off was to be made at the museum that night, Shawna asked me, "Where'd you learn that?"

"I saw the text on your cell phone."

"Oh shit!"

"Shut up!" Kevin snarled.

The Mounties let us go, but asked that we drop in at the detachment at nine the next morning to make an official statement. As we walked back to our car, Anton remarked ruefully, "I never thought of the RCMP last night. Of course. They are the ones we should have reported the shooting to.

We left with a feeling of a job well done.

Sgt. Tucker joined the RCMP officer who questioned us about the incidents of Saturday night, and when we described Anton's experience of the previous night, he listened with intense interest. I saw him exchange a brief glance with the RCMP officer. After the Mountie left to get our statements transcribed, Tucker remained to talk to us.

"I was very interested in your adventure, Dr. Schild. We have been trying to get something definite on this young man you know of as Billy. His father, William Akers, is a city councillor, as you may know, and that means he is in effect our boss. The city hires, and can fire, the chief of police, and Akers has indicated he will try to have the city do so if we don't 'leave my son alone' as he puts it. But the city has no jurisdiction over the RCMP. They may be able to resolve our problem for us since the hoodoos are outside the city, and policing that area falls on the RCMP. Dr. McKinnon, are you sure that the bicycle you saw belonged to Billy?"

"I'm sure. But of course, neither of us could see the man clearly enough to identify him."

Tucker nodded. "You think he uses the hoodoos as another drop-off point."

"Yes."

"But you can't be sure he is the person who sent the e-mail to the girl, Shawna."

"No."

"Well, it might interest you to know that those two broke down when they were questioned and told us everything. And they named Billy as the one who supplies them."

"I'm glad to hear it," I said.

"The problem, though, is that Billy gets the stuff from someone higher up in the chain. We can arrest him and those two kids, but the next person up the chain will just find someone else and some other places to distribute the drugs."

"I suppose so."

"Anyway, thanks for your help. But tell me why you took it upon yourselves to do it."

"They were using my clinic."

"I see that."

"And," Anton went on, "we wanted to find out whether there was any indication at all that Jon Mendel was involved. Was there?"

"No. There wasn't. I asked those kids whether he was one of their customers. They had never heard of him."

I heaved a great sigh of relief, and Anton had a grin on his face.

CHAPTER TWENTY

The funeral was set for Tuesday, and on Monday we got a call from Bishop Ormond asking us if we could pick him up at the airport when the early morning plane came in. He would take a late flight to Calgary on Monday evening, and get the early one to Drayford on Tuesday morning.

Anton met me at the clinic when I finished work Tuesday morning, and we went to the airport. The plane was just unloading its passengers. The bishop emerged carrying a bag containing his vestments. He asked us if we had eaten breakfast before coming to meet him and since we hadn't, and neither had he, we stopped at a downtown café that had been recommended to us. After we had ordered, we began to discuss the investigation.

"Our local paper doesn't have any news about Drayford's murder. Has anything new happened?" Bishop Ormond asked.

"Not much," I replied. "We see the police around the campus all the time, and I know that they have talked to many of the students, the faculty members and staff. As far as I know we're still suspects, though Sgt. Tucker is friendly with us. But he doesn't tell us who he suspects."

"He has to be cautious," Anton volunteered. "If he says the wrong thing, it could get him into trouble."

The bishop nodded. "I assume that Mrs. Mendel is staying for the funeral."

"She is. We've spoken to her a couple of times. She's not staying at the house. I think she's staying at a hotel. She said she would be leaving after the funeral to go back to Vancouver."

"I'll have to get in touch with her this morning. I assume that the local church office will know where I can find her. I'll call them when they open."

Our food was served and conversation ceased until we finished eating. I had an idea I wanted to try out on the bishop, but I knew he wouldn't like it.

"People are always talking about love triangles, when one person is married to another, but is interested in a third person. But that isn't really a triangle, it's a V."

"Would you explain that?" the bishop asked.

I took a napkin, pulled out my pen, and diagramed what I was talking about as I talked. "A, here, is married to B." I drew a line between the letters. "But A is also friendly with another person, C, who responds." I drew another line from A to C. "That's not a triangle, it's a V."

The bishop and Anton nodded.

"But let's take the situation with the Mendels and Niall Raymond. A, Leah Mendel, is married to B, Jon. Gossip has it that Leah is interested in C, Niall."

"But…" Anton interrupted.

"I know what you're going to say, that she really wasn't. Be patient and hear me out."

Anton sank back into a waiting attitude.

"To go on, here we have the V, where B is married to A who is reported to be interested in C. But C isn't interested in

A. He, Niall, is interested in B, Jon." I connected them with a line on my diagram. "That is a real triangle."

While they thought that over, I went on. "Suppose that it was Niall who came back that night and Jon let him in. Jon had changed back into his swim trunks before he received Leah's call, planning to go for another swim. Maybe Niall propositioned him, and Jon told him he wasn't interested and turned his back on Niall, walking out to the pool. Niall, feeling jilted, became very angry, and as he followed Jon, he detoured into the kitchen and pulled a knife out of the rack. When Jon told him to leave, Niall's anger got the better of him and he attacked Jon, causing the wound that knocked Jon into the pool." I decided that I wouldn't describe what happened after that. Enough horror is enough.

The bishop sighed. "I hope you aren't going to talk about your idea anywhere else. Even if it is true, and I'm not agreeing that it is, think of the distress that suggestion would cause to Jon's parents, who are a very devout elderly couple in an assisted living facility. It's not fair to subject them to that type of supposition. And think of the distress it would cause to Jon's wife. I think that what is needed is a concrete piece of evidence, rather than a supposition that is pure conjecture. I think you should leave the investigation to the police and remain quiet about your idea."

Anton remarked, "I agree with the bishop. It's not our responsibility to solve this murder. I think the local police are very competent and will eventually come up with the answer."

"I guess you're right," I had to admit.

Speak of the devil! The door opened and Sgt. Tucker entered. He looked around the busy café, which was quite crowded. I motioned to him. "Come over here and sit with us." Bishop Ormond moved over to give him room.

Tucker called to the waitress, "The usual."

"Coming right up," she replied.

He sank into the cushioned seat of the booth with a sigh. He looked tired. "Rough night?" I asked.

"Early morning more like. Vandals were caught effacing one wall of the Convention Centre. We caught them and made them go back and clean it up. It's hard work scrubbing fresh paint off, but we made them remove every last bit. They may remember that the next time they think about spraying rude slogans on a public building."

Tucker's breakfast arrived. "The usual" turned out to be ham and eggs, sunny side up, whole-wheat toast and hash browns. Tucker dug in, eating rapidly and efficiently. Anton leaned forward.

"Sergeant, I have another question I'd like to ask you."

"My, you're an inquisitive young man Dr. Schild."

"I'm a scientist. Inquisitiveness is programmed into us."

"Okay. What is it you want to know this time?"

"I've been wondering about Jon's next door neighbour. You say he vouched for us when we left Jon's house that night. What about him? He seemed like a logical suspect, but we haven't heard anything about him in your news releases."

"You're right. We did look into his movements that night in detail. But he's accounted for at the relevant time. He must have walked back up the street after Dr. Mendel's visitor had entered the house. He says that he didn't see anyone. He got home about ten minutes after eleven and his wife verifies that. She was just in the process of answering the phone. It was their daughter, who is with one of those relief organizations. They were sent to somewhere in the Middle East and had just arrived there and she hadn't figured out the time zone differences yet; that's why she called so late. They talked for a little over half an hour. We have verified the call. That pretty much excludes him from being the one who stabbed Dr. Mendel."

"I see. Thanks."

In the following silence, an idea suddenly popped into my mind. If I'd been a character in a comic strip, there would have been a balloon over my head with a light bulb in it. The idea was that sudden.

"Sgt. Tucker, are you a morning person or a night person?"

"What do you mean?"

"Do you leap out of bed in the morning, ready to get started on your day's work, or do you have to drag yourself out of bed and only liven up at the end of the day?"

"I usually don't have any choice. I go to work whenever I'm needed, and finish whenever I can." He went back to his ham and eggs.

"Anton here is a morning person. He's up at five in the morning, without fail, and goes on a run or bike ride around the campus. On the first morning we were here, a Sunday, he went for a run and stopped to meet all the maintenance workers, who are out early to get their tasks done before classes start. He ended up at the Dragon Fountain and talked to the guys who were cleaning it.

"On the other hand, our neighbour, Niall Raymond, never gets up before nine o'clock in the morning. He's a night person. He is out on the town until the small hours of the morning. I see him downtown most nights when I'm at work. He has been here since the college opened three years ago, but I'll bet that he still doesn't know that when the fountain shuts off on Saturday night, it also automatically drains itself, so the workers can clean it in the morning. So he wouldn't know that throwing a bloody knife into the pool wouldn't do any good, because the pool would soon be dry and the maintenance men would be out first thing in the morning. Besides, I'm sure it was just a little after midnight when he came home that night, and the first thing he did was start the washer."

Tucker listened intently, his fork poised between the plate and his mouth. When I finished, he gulped the forkful of food and hastily shoveled the rest of his meal into his mouth. As he rose from his seat, he took a last swig of coffee. He pulled a twenty from his billfold and threw it on the counter beside the till, calling to the waitress, "Keep the change." He was out the door like a shot.

The waitress approached us with a refill of coffee. "He does that all the time. He's always being called away in the middle of his meal. I just take out my tip, and the next time he comes in, I don't charge him as much."

We declined the coffee, since we were ready to leave. As Bishop Ormond slid out of the booth, he smiled at me and said, "Well done, Dr. McKinnon."

When we arrived home after delivering Bishop Ormond to the local church, we found Niall Raymond's townhouse swarming with police. Another neighbour told us that the police had taken Raymond, handcuffed and screaming threats, to a waiting police car. As we watched, cops came out of the house carrying plastic bags that appeared to contain blue jeans and T-shirts as well as a pair of leather-soled loafers. They remained in the house for some time, and on leaving strung crime scene tape around the property.

CHAPTER TWENTY-ONE

We arrived early for the funeral and saw Bishop Ormond supervising the removal of a black frontal from the altar, and its replacement with a white one. I could remember, at a time when I was very small, being taken to a funeral where the liturgical colour was black. But more recently the Anglican Church has used white for funerals, the occasion being a celebration of the life of the deceased. This indeed must be an old traditional church that was way behind the modern concepts of Anglican worship. I thought that we might as well skip a visit to it, and start attending the Lutheran one on a regular basis.

Ormond appeared in full bishop's vestments, which should have made the locals happy. Some bishops these days don't dress up that way. The bishop of my diocese in Ontario wore a regular priest's chasuble when he came to visit my hometown church, the only thing showing that he was a bishop being his mitre.

Leah Mendel was the only mourner sitting in the front pew, reserved for family members of the deceased. Jon's elderly parents had been unable to attend, due to their failing health. The two wannabe girlfriends were there, sitting one row back from the pew reserved for the family, but on opposite sides of the church. Leah was calm and composed, and followed the service in the Book of Alternative Services attentively. The locals may not have approved of the use of this rite rather than the one in the Book of Common Prayer, but this was Jon's funeral, not for one of their members. The funeral service was impressive, as Anglican funerals can be.

When we left the church, we ran into Sgt. Tucker. He seemed much more at ease than he had that morning. He verified that Niall Raymond had been arrested, but claimed his innocence, as he would. He also claimed that he had no interest in Leah Mendel.

"But we'll break him down with time. That must be his motive, but it will be hard to prove. The only other motive we could come up with was that he was involved somehow in drugs, but we've eliminated that."

Anton gave me a sidelong glance, probably to see whether I was going to break out into a theory that Niall's interest was in Jon, not Leah. No way was I going to do that. They had physical evidence now, and motive wasn't necessary to prove a crime. I'd leave that subject strictly alone.

"I saw you removing clothes and shoes from Niall's house. Did you find anything on them?" I asked.

"We did. You will hear all about it on the news tonight, so I might as well tell you. He had washed the jeans and shirt he was wearing, but we found traces of blood anyway. And the shoes were a dead giveaway. He cleaned them and used brown shoe polish liberally. But he apparently failed to realize that, though he did not walk in the blood after it had sprayed around, he had also gotten blood on the soles from stepping on the victim's fingers. The uppers were sewed to the sole, and at every stitch there was a veritable trap for blood and flesh. The blood is the same type as the victim's, type B, which is much less common than types O or A, but isn't rare either. When we get the DNA results, we'll know for certain."

"How did you know what clothes to look for? You only took one pair of jeans, as far as I could tell."

"We asked around among the students. We found one young man who was in one of Raymond's classes, who not only saw him downtown that night, about ten or ten thirty, but also talked to him. He said Raymond was wearing blue jeans and a black T-shirt. He only has one pair of blue jeans, but has several black shirts with various designs on them. We took all of them, but only found blood on one.

"Then, the officer who said he saw Raymond downtown that night, got to thinking about it and figuring out where he had seen Raymond and what time it was. He was able to figure the time as about one. He says Raymond was wearing chinos and a plaid shirt."

"And I heard him start his washer about twelve fifteen."

"There you are! We've got our man, thanks to you. You will probably get a thank you letter from the Chief. He likes to thank people for their help.

"By the way, you should have heard Mrs. Mendel when she was facing Raymond. She told him in no uncertain terms that she had never had any interest in him, and that if he killed her husband she hoped he would rot in hell. She really let him have it. Wow! You should have heard her."

I tried to visualize the quiet, demure woman I had met as the virago he was describing. I guess when you're angry enough you can let yourself go.

Tim MacQuarrie had been hanging around while we talked to Tucker. I had seen him in church with a large group of students. Apparently the entire class from last year's course with Jon Mendel had come to the funeral. I wondered if Tim had rounded them all up. He seemed to be a type of young man who would be a leader. When Tucker left, he came over and spoke to us.

"That was a wonderful service. I've never been to a funeral like that. And I had a chance to meet Leah and tell her how much I appreciated Dr. Mendel."

"That was good of you Tim," Anton replied.

"Anyway," Tim went on, "I wanted to let you know I talked to Dr. Hopkins and showed him the programme I was working on, and he told me to go ahead with it, and he asked me if I'd like to help teach the class. He said I couldn't be paid for it, but he'd arrange for a substantial bursary to help me next semester and next year."

"That's wonderful Tim. See, ask and you shall receive! I thought Charlie Hopkins would be impressed with your work."

"And Dr. Hopkins said he thought I should apply to one of the universities, after I graduate here, and do graduate work in math, working on formation of a programme of practical math for high schools and universities. I'm sort of overwhelmed."

"Tim, I'm happy for you. I hope you seriously consider it."

"I called my Mum and Dad. I didn't know how they would react. I thought they might be disappointed, because they expected me to come home and eventually take over the ranch. I'm the first person in my family to go to college, and they expected me to come back with new ideas on how to improve the ranch."

"How did they take it?"

"Actually, they were really happy for me. They think of it as an honour, and are proud of their son. And besides, my little sister will be starting here at Drayford next year, and I know she'd like to go back to the ranch. So they'll still have someone to keep it in the family when they have to give up working it."

We both congratulated Tim. It was a ray of sunshine in an otherwise gloomy day.

CHAPTER TWENTY-TWO

Several weeks later, we were relaxing in our living room with mugs of mulled wine, watching the gathering dusk and the first flakes of the initial snowfall of the winter. We discussed the murder of our friend, the preliminary inquiry having resulted in Niall Raymond being bound over to stand trial for Jon Mendel's murder. Anton had given evidence about the identification of the knife and the finding of Jon's body. I was not called to testify about hearing him come home and wash his clothes because they had better evidence from the people who had seen him downtown. That subject exhausted, we sat in silence for a while before Anton asked me, "You're not really happy here, are you?"

I had to think for a minute before answering. "If you're talking about my work, it has its problems. Otherwise, there are many things about Drayford that I like. And I know that you have found your calling. You are a natural teacher, and you enjoy it. That makes me happy. Why do you ask?"

"The latest issue of our technical journal came today and I was looking through the want ads. The position at the lab in Regina is still being advertised. That means that they haven't found anyone else. I was wondering if I should inquire about whether they would still be interested in me."

That was a stunner. I thought Anton was really happy at Drayford. I suggested tentatively, "Why don't you contact them and ask?"

"Look, if I'm going to put in my request again, I'm going to have to be serious about it. I can't wait till they accept me and then say I've decided to stay in Drayford. If I apply again, I have to want to go."

"Well, do you?"

"I'm not sure. They have far better equipment and get big grants for their work. On the other hand, I have the opportunity here to build something from scratch. If I can do it, the equipment and the grants will follow in due time. It's a challenge. But I won't be happy here unless you are."

"Speaking of challenges, I've been considering the challenge of trying to make this emergency clinic work. I'm not satisfied with the way I have to run it now. It needs a lot of changes. I've been thinking that what I'd really like is to buy out the other vets and run it my own way. But that would require a huge outlay of cash. I'd need at least two other vets to go into it with me, as well as more staff. And that would cost a lot more. We would have to run it as a regular veterinary practice during the day, and then offer fulltime emergency care. Or run it as a specialty practice during the day, inviting specialists to come from Calgary or Edmonton one day a week. To do that, we'd have to provide some specialty equipment for them, which would be another expense. I can't see it as feasible for several years yet. I doubt if I could get that kind of a loan until I've established a good credit rating and am earning a lot more than I am at the present time."

"So you think it would be years down the road before you can do what you really want to."

"Oh, it's not *that* bad!"

"Isn't it?"

"Let's talk about you," I remarked. "You like it here and you are a natural teacher."

"I come from four generations of teachers. It's in my genes."

"That's what I mean. You belong here, teaching students. You'll probably be an assistant professor next year, and maybe in a few years have tenure. And if your work in the lab pans out, the grants will come. You should really think twice before giving that up."

"I like it, yes. But there are a couple of students who are taking my class merely to disrupt it. When they won't listen to my answers to their accusations, I just try to go on with my lecture, and if they keep disrupting, it's the other students who tell them to shut up. At the lab in Regina I'd be working all the time with people who have the same interest as I have. Besides, there is a possibility of teaching a course or two at the University of Regina or the University of Saskatchewan in Saskatoon. Also Saskatchewan has the vet school. Have you ever considered a teaching position?"

I grunted. "I'm no teacher."

"How do you know? Have you ever tried it?"

"Aren't we getting off the subject? I don't want to be in Saskatoon if you are in Regina."

"Granted," he admitted, "but it seems to me that the kind of vet practice that you are interested in would be easier to set up in a larger city. Has anyone done it?"

"Oh, sure. There's one in Calgary, and one in Victoria, BC. And I think there's something like that in Regina. They were advertising for another vet several months ago."

"Maybe you could get on there. Even if that position is taken, there may be another one open one of these days. You could ask."

There followed a long period of silence, broken at last by Anton. "This isn't getting us anywhere. What we need to do is for each of us to make a list of all the reasons we would like to stay here, and another of all the reasons we might want to leave. Then compare them."

"That sounds like a good idea," I agreed. "I'll get some paper and pens."

When I returned with two scratch pads and two pens, Anton had another suggestion. "We should stick to listing our own personal reasons for either staying or leaving, and not try to think of what the other person might want."

"Agreed."

It took us nearly an hour to compile our lists. We refreshed our drinks. I brought out some snacks. Anton got up and stretched a couple of times. Silence reigned. It was the same atmosphere as I remembered when taking final exams. We really wanted to do this right. Eventually we both decided we'd done as good a job as we could and got together to compare results. Anton took another sheet from his pad and wrote the headings 'Stay' and 'Leave.' We added up the results on our lists and combined them, adding the totals for each of the two categories. My list for 'Leave' was longer than the one for 'Stay,' but Anton's was the opposite. When totaled, the two columns were almost dead even.

"Well, that didn't do much good," Anton complained.

"I don't know. I think it clarified things in our heads."

"Maybe you're right," he agreed, "but it still doesn't give us an answer. What do we do now?"

"Flip a coin," I said facetiously.

Anton fished in his pocket for a quarter and held it out to me saying, like a football referee, "This is a head, and this is a tail. Your call."

"Heads we stay, tails we leave."

He flipped the coin expertly into the air. It turned over and over and finally plopped onto the rug in the centre of the living room. We eagerly bent over to look at it. Too eagerly. Our heads crashed together with a cracking sound and we staggered upright, each holding a hand over our respective foreheads.

"Let's try that again," Anton said weakly.

"Carefully," I replied.

We bent over again, slowly and carefully, and stared at the coin on the floor.

The End

About the Author

Carolyn Dale is a pen name of mystery author Anne Barton.

Anne Barton is a retired veterinarian and flight instructor. In her retirement, she has taken up writing mystery novels. She has also written one autobiographical book and numerous articles and short stories. Her short story won the Bloody Words Crime Writers' Conference contest in 2001 and is published in Bloody Words, The Anthology.

Born in Drumheller, Alberta, she grew up in Northern Idaho, returned to Canada, and now lives in the beautiful Okanagan Valley in British Columbia, where she is deeply involved with Habitat for Humanity and her Anglican Church work – that is, when she isn't riding horses or curling.

www.annebartonmysteries.ca
www.mysterycarolyndale.ca